Hooples On The Highway

Other Avon Camelot Books by
Stephen Manes

THE BOY WHO TURNED INTO A TV SET

STEPHEN MANES is a versatile and popular author and screenwriter. He has published more than twenty books for kids, including *The Boy Who Turned into a TV Set, Be a Perfect Person in Just Three Days!, The Hooples' Haunted House,* and *Life is No Fair!* He lives in Riverdale, New York. When not writing with the help of a computer named Bambi, he is often found wandering down the highways of the world.

Hooples On The Highway

By Stephen Manes

AN AVON CAMELOT BOOK

AVON BOOKS
A division of
The Hearst Corporation
1790 Broadway
New York, New York 10019

The Coward, McCann & Geoghegan, Inc. edition contains the following
Library of Congress Cataloging in Publication Data:

Manes, Stephen. Hooples on the highway.

SUMMARY: A seemingly simple automobile trip to Philadelphia is fraught
with adventures for the Hoople family.
[1. Vacations—Fiction.   2. Family life—Fiction]
II. Title.
PZ7.M31264Ho   [Fic]   78-1710

First Camelot Printing, July 1985

For Esther

1

"Rise and shine, everybody!" Alvin hollered as he bounced up and down on his parents' bed. "Vacation time!"

"Criminentlies, Alvin!" grumped Mr. Hoople, waking up and fumbling for the clock. "It's five in the morning! Even the sun has better sense than to get up at this hour!"

"But you said you wanted to get an early start."

"Early, yes," Mrs. Hoople yawned, "but this is ridiculous!"

"I'm wide awake," Alvin insisted. "Tell you what. I'll go down and fix breakfast for everybody."

"Alvin, go back to bed," Dad grumbled. "We're going to eat breakfast on the road."

"Wouldn't it be more sanitary to eat it on a table?" Alvin asked.

Mom and Dad groaned. The last thing they wanted to hear at five in the morning was one of Alvin's jokes.

As they were pleading with Alvin to let them get some rest, his little sister Annie shuffled into the room, rubbing the sleep from her eyes. "When's breakfast?'' she yelled, waving her favorite stuffed animal around by the leg. ''Lambie's hungry.''

''Now *I'm* wide awake,'' Mom sighed. ''May as well get up, Andy.''

''Phooey,'' Dad muttered as he got out of bed and peeked between the curtains at the darkness outside. ''Fine vacation this is starting out to be.''

Alvin couldn't agree more. He'd been waiting a whole month, and now the big day was finally here. By evening they'd be in Philadelphia. Alvin had never been there before. He could hardly wait to see the Liberty Bell and Independence Hall and Benjamin Franklin's house, and especially the United States Mint, where the government makes coins. Somebody had told him that they gave out free samples if you went on the right day, and even though Mom and Dad claimed it wasn't true, Alvin wanted to go and see for himself.

But as far as Alvin was concerned, the best thing of all about this trip would be tonight's Phillies baseball game. Alvin was the biggest Phillies fan in Sherwood Forest, New York. Most of his friends rooted for the Mets or the Yankees, but Alvin's dad and mom had grown up in Philadelphia, so Alvin rooted for the Phils. And though he'd watched them on television often, he'd never yet seen them in person. Tonight would be special.

But that wasn't all: Tonight was Bat Night. It only happened once a year. As it said on his Phillies schedule, every youngster fourteen and under would receive a free baseball bat with autographs of all the Phillies stars. It was a souvenir to be treasured. You couldn't buy it anywhere. You had to be at tonight's game to get one. And Alvin would be there, rooting for the Phils in Section 324, Row J, Seat 22. The tickets had come in the mail, and Alvin had memorized his seat number. He'd be right behind home plate. He might even catch a foul ball. It would be the beginning of the best vacation ever.

In fact, everything about Philadelphia sounded great, except for Cousin Marty, who lived there. Alvin's family was going to stay with Marty's family, and Marty was a fat creep. The last time he'd visited the Hooples, Marty had broken two of Alvin's model planes and his space shuttle without even apologizing. He hated baseball. He cheated at games. And he told so many fibs, you never could believe a word he said. Come to think of it, Alvin seemed to remember it was Cousin Marty who'd told him about the free samples at the Mint.

But Alvin didn't intend to let Cousin Marty or anybody else spoil his fun. Just being up this early was exciting. Alvin pressed his nose to the window screen and listened carefully. It was quiet outside, except for the chirps of some early-rising crickets. Across the way, all the houses were dark. Maybe the Hooples were the only ones up in the entire neighborhood. Alvin thought it'd be fun to yell out the window at the top of his lungs and see what happened, but he decided Dad and the neighbors might object.

Usually Alvin dawdled in the bathroom, but today he washed his face, brushed his teeth, and combed his hair in a jiffy. Usually he was a slowpoke getting dressed, but today he was ready in a flash. He rooted around in his sock drawer and found the five crumpled dollar bills and eighty-six cents in change he'd saved especially for this trip. Then he gathered up his first baseman's mitt, his Phillies cap, his shoe box full of baseball cards, his jar of lightning bugs, and his collection of road maps, carried them all downstairs, and dumped them on the couch.

"Are you really taking all that stuff?" Mom asked him as she finished locking the front windows.

"Sure. Is there anything I can do to help?" he asked, secretly hoping there wasn't.

"Check with your father. He's out in the garage."

Mr. Hoople certainly looked as if he could use some help. The car's trunk was stuffed to the brim with luggage, and when he tried to close it, the lid popped open like a jack-in-the-box. He hummed thoughtfully, scratched his head, shifted the suitcases, and slammed the trunk lid hard. It popped right back open again and nearly socked him in the jaw. He moved the luggage around once more and gave the lid a mighty slam. This time it almost whacked him in the nose when it popped back up again.

Alvin giggled. "Alvin," Dad said, frustrated, "instead of laughing, come here and give me a hand."

Alvin applauded.

Dad scowled. Another rotten joke before breakfast was more than he could bear. "Come on, Alvin," he pleaded.

"What do you want me to do?"

"Help me shut this thing. But watch out for your fingers. Now, I'll count three. Ready?"

Alvin nodded.

"All right! One . . . two . . . THREE!" Dad

pushed down on one side, Alvin pushed down on the other, and the trunk snapped shut.

Dad smiled. "Good work."

Alvin grinned proudly. "Anytime."

The trunk popped open again.

"Once more!" Dad cried determinedly. On the count of three, he and Alvin slammed the lid shut. This time Dad tugged on it afterward to make sure it would really stay closed. And as he and Alvin went inside, Dad gave the trunk a dirty look just to make sure it wouldn't try anything funny behind his back.

"Well, I think we're almost ready," said Mom, looking over her list of things to do. "Does anybody have to go to the bathroom before we leave?"

"Not me," said Alvin.

"Me neither," said Dad. "How about you, Annie?"

"No, and Lambie neither."

"Then I'll meet you all at the car," Mom said. "I want to check the faucets upstairs and make sure they aren't dripping." Alvin thought how funny it would be if the bathtub overflowed while they were gone and they came back to find the stairs had turned into a waterfall. It'd be the marvel of the neighborhood. He could even charge admission. But somehow he knew that kind of thing seemed to happen only in books, except for the time Mom's washing machine overflowed and turned into a Suds Monster crawling across the basement floor.

"Can I sit up front?" Alvin asked his father when they got to the car.

"Not until I've had my first cup of coffee," Dad replied.

11

"But the navigator always sits up front," Alvin protested.

"Not when he wakes the pilot up at five in the morning," Dad said.

"Can I sit up front?" Annie asked.

"Doesn't Lambie like it better in the back?"

"Sometimes he gets carsick," she replied, but crawled into the backseat anyhow.

"Stop squirming!" Alvin told her as he helped her with her seat belt.

"Belt Lambie in, too!" she insisted.

Alvin gave her a funny look.

"Please, Alvin!" she begged. "I want him to be safe."

Alvin explained that there were only two belts in the backseat, both reserved for humans. Annie hugged Lambie tight. "Don't worry," she told him. "I'll protect you."

"I wonder what's keeping your mother," Dad remarked.

Just then she burst through the door with a little suitcase. "You forgot Annie's bag, Andy," she scowled, and headed for the trunk.

"Wait a minute, Alice! Hold on!" Dad yelled as Mom put her key in the trunk. "No! Hold it!" If she opened that trunk, they'd never get it closed again. Dad jumped out of the car and tried to stop her.

Too late! Mom turned the key, and the trunk flew open. Dad closed his eyes and shuddered.

Mom pretended she didn't notice. She moved the luggage around, made room for Annie's suitcase, and ever so gently shut the trunk. "Bet it won't stay,'' said Dad, tugging hard on the lid. But it did. He gave Mom a peck on the cheek.

They got into the front, and Dad started the car. "Away we go!" he boomed.

"Hooray!" Alvin cheered.

"Hoorah!" Mom sighed.

"Lambie and I have to use the toilet," Annie announced.

Alvin glared at her. "Why didn't you do that before?" he complained.

"Because," Annie replied, with a look that made it clear there was nothing more to discuss.

So Dad turned off the engine, and Mom unlocked the house and took Annie and Lambie to the bathroom, and Dad and Alvin waited impatiently. Mom and Annie finally came back again.

As the car started rolling down the driveway, Annie shouted, "I'm carsick!" Nobody paid her any attention.

2

A big red sun was just sneaking over the horizon as Alvin watched the neighborhood go past the car windows. Behind him, the Hooples' house got smaller and smaller in the distance, and when they turned the corner it disappeared entirely. They passed the gas station, the fire station, and the shopping center, and at the traffic light Dad turned onto the highway. They were on their way at last!

"I'm hungry," Annie declared.

At least she isn't carsick anymore, Alvin thought with a sigh of relief. He never forgot the time she was carsick all over his pants, and he wasn't in the mood for a repeat performance.

"We want to get on the road a ways before we stop for breakfast," Dad told Annie. "Think you can hold out a little while?"

"No!" cried Annie. "I want to eat *there!*" And she pointed to Chick's Chicken Kitchen, where the family went out to dinner now and then.

"I really don't think you'd like fried chicken for breakfast," said Mom.

"I certainly would," Annie replied.

14

"Well, they're not open now anyway, so I guess you'll have to try it some other time," Mom told her.

"Oh," said Annie, truly sorry to hear it. "But I'm still hungry."

"How about a song?" Dad suggested. "That'll take your mind off your stomach till we eat."

"What song?" Annie asked suspiciously.

"Any song your little heart desires," Dad replied.

"I know a good one," said Annie, and she began to sing:

> Do your own thing
> At Wienie King.
> Do your own thing
> At Wienie King.
> Have a foot-long frank
> On a sesame bun,
> Go crazy with onions
> Or have mustard and none,
> Eat it right here
> Or on the run,
> Yes, do your thing
> At Wienie King.

"And I'm still hungry," she insisted.

"Tough," said Dad.

They passed three diners and four cafés and any number of places advertising "Fine Food," but Dad wasn't ready to stop yet. Annie was getting hungrier by the minute and reminded everybody every chance she got. Alvin's stomach was beginning to rumble, and even Mom wouldn't've minded some nourishment, but Dad had his heart set on a place called the

15

"Copper Skillet," which he said had excellent food at very reasonable prices.

So the whole family was relieved when they saw a sign with a big picture of a frying pan and the words "COPPER SKILLET—HOME COOKING—FIVE MILES." They were delighted when they passed an even bigger frying pan on a sign that read "COPPER SKILLET—HOME COOKING—TWO MILES." They were positively drooling when they saw the biggest frying pan yet on a sign that read "SLOW DOWN!—JUST ONE MORE MILE TO COPPER SKILLET—HOME COOKING." And when they spotted an enormous frying pan with two superjumbo fried eggs atop a huge "COPPER SKILLET" sign above the restaurant, they'd've jumped up and down if it hadn't been for their seat belts.

"That's funny," Dad muttered as they drove into the parking lot. "There's nobody else here."

Alvin noticed a tiny skillet-shaped sign taped inside the glass door. " 'Sorry we missed you!' " he read. " 'Closed for vacation till August 23.' "

"What're we gonna do now?" Alvin asked politely.

"Yeah!" wailed Annie. "What're we gonna do now?"

"We'll stop at the very next restaurant we come to," said Dad. "Does that suit you?"

"No," grumped Annie. "I'm hungry now."

"Then munch on Lambie for a while," Dad grumbled as he steered the car back onto the highway. He was rather disappointed, and explained again how the Copper Skillet served your eggs in the very frying pan they were cooked in.

16

Mom wasn't impressed. "Eggs are eggs," said she, "and if we don't get something to eat pretty soon, my tummy's going to run off and leave me for someone who treats it better."

"Mine, too," Annie chimed in.

The next restaurant they came to had a red neon sign that blinked "GAS—EATS—GAS—EATS."

"I'll say," laughed Alvin, only half joking. Attached to a filling station, the eatery looked so filthy even Annie was willing to pass it up.

"They probably serve their eggs in your hubcaps," Mom commented.

Alvin consulted his map. "We should find something soon," he said. "We're coming into a little town."

Sure enough, a mile or so down the road a sign welcomed them to Marvelous Muckleburg, Home of the Muckleburg Muskrats Championship Marching Band. Alvin didn't see any marching muskrats, but his eagle eye spotted a "Coffee Shop" sign dangling from an awning up ahead. "And that," Dad proclaimed, "is where we shall eat."

They all went in. The friendly blond hostess showed them to a booth by the window. "Enjoy your breakfast," she said cheerfully.

"I could eat a horse!" Annie declared. "I could eat a bear! I bet I could eat a elephant!"

"You came in on the wrong day, I'm sorry to say. Horse, bear, and elephant are the Wednesday specials," the hostess said, winking, and went back to tend the cash register.

While Dad and Alvin looked over their menus, Mom read hers to Annie. Every time Mom mentioned something, Annie said she wanted it, except for the stewed prunes, to which she made a very ugly face. So her breakfast might have consisted of orange juice, tomato juice, grapefruit juice, milk, Rice Krispies, Post Toasties, oatmeal, sausage, ham, bacon, home-fried potatoes, pancakes, waffles, French toast, jam, marmalade, English muffins, and one, two, or three eggs any style if Dad hadn't proposed a compromise. "Annie," he said, "why don't I decide on a nice breakfast for you, and then if you're still hungry, you can order something else."

"Okay," Annie agreed.

Mom, Dad, and Alvin told the waitress what they wanted, and then Dad ordered for Annie. "Our daughter would like a glass of orange juice, some bacon and a scrambled egg, and a glass of milk, please."

"No, I wouldn't," said Annie.

"What *do* you want, then?" Mom asked, a little bit annoyed.

"I want to order for myself." Annie turned to the waitress and thought each item over very carefully. "I would like a scrambled egg . . . some bacon . . . and a glass of milk, please. And some orange juice."

"Yes, ma'am," the waitress said, and scurried toward the kitchen.

"Did I do okay?" Annie asked.

"You did fine," said Dad, smiling.

"I didn't order for Lambie," Annie said, "but he can have some of mine."

It wasn't long before the food arrived, and everyone agreed it was delicious. Alvin particularly liked having cantaloupe instead of the orange juice he usu-

18

ally got at home, and as a special treat, he and Annie got to split the maraschino cherry from Dad's grapefruit. Annie kindly offered Lambie some of her eggs, but he wasn't hungry, so she let him sniff the plastic flowers.

Alvin experimented with various combinations of the honey and three different syrups that came in neat little pitchers with his huge stack of pancakes. Eventually, the maple flowed into the blueberry, and the honey trickled down into the apricot, and they all blended together in one big honeymapleblueberry-apricot moat around the Isle of Pancakes. Alvin decided that combination was the best of all. Dad snitched a piece of Alvin's sausage, but Alvin reminded him he was supposed to be on a diet and made him give it back.

"I guess you didn't care much for your breakfast," Dad kidded, staring in astonishment at Alvin's empty plate.

"Nope," Alvin chuckled, licking the last driblets of syrup from the corners of his mouth. After that huge meal, he was so full he couldn't possibly eat another bite—unless maybe somebody offered him some chocolate ice cream.

"I don't know where you put it all," Mom marveled.

"In his stomach, silly," said Annie.

"Did you enjoy your breakfast?" Dad asked her.

"Lambie and I both enjoyed it," she replied as Mom wiped her milk-and-orange-juice moustache. "What's for dessert?"

Nothing was for dessert. Everybody went to the rest rooms. Alvin enjoyed rubbing his hands together under the warm air of the electric dryer. It felt nice and toasty and seemed a lot more sanitary than towels, even though it took longer.

While Dad was paying the hostess, Alvin noticed a toothpick dispenser beside the cash register. He pushed the white button marked "PUSH." Two little wooden fingers slipped inside the dispenser and emerged with a toothpick. "I want one, too," said Annie. Alvin pushed the button again and handed her a toothpick of her very own.

"I'll just give that one to Lambie," she said, sticking it in the animals ear. "I want to do it myself." But Annie was just too short to reach the button. She stretched and stood up on tiptoe, but she still couldn't reach. So she jumped up and grabbed for the push button.

Crash! The whole dispenser fell to the floor, and hundreds of smooth round toothpicks rolled every which way across the linoleum. The hostess shook her head in dismay. Dad picked up the dispenser (which fortunately wasn't broken) and glared at Annie sternly. "It was an accident," she whimpered, looking almost as sheepish as Lambie. "I'll pick them up."

"Every last one," said Mom. She and Alvin stooped down to help.

"I'm very sorry," Dad told the hostess. "I'll be glad to pay for the toothpicks."

"But we're picking them up," Annie protested. "They're not broken."

"Or sanitary, either," said Alvin, shaking his head.

The cashier forced a smile. "Accidents will hap-

20

pen,'' she told Mr. Hoople. ''Why don't you take the toothpicks home with you? I once knew a fellow who built a whole circus out of 'em. Maybe your kids can do the same.'' And she gave Alvin a little bag to put the toothpicks into.

''You're very understanding,'' said Dad.

''Got three of my own at home,'' the hostess beamed.

''Three toothpicks?'' Annie wondered aloud.

''Three *delightful* children,'' said the hostess, though the way she said ''delightful'' made Alvin doubt she meant it.

Annie tried hard, but she wasn't much help with the toothpicks. She picked them up with her right hand and put them into her left, but her hand was so little that for every toothpick she put into it, another (and often two) would fall out. She didn't even notice, so if it hadn't been for Mom and Alvin, Annie might've been there picking up toothpicks all summer long.

''Sorry we caused you all this trouble,'' Mom told the hostess once the wooden slivers were finally in the bag.

''No trouble at all,'' the hostess replied, almost as if she meant it. ''Come in again next time you're out our way.''

''We certainly will,'' said Dad. As he led the family toward the door, his foot came down on a stray toothpick, and his legs went out from under him. He nearly fell right on top of his son, but alert Alvin jumped out of the way in the nick of time, and Dad sat down hard on the linoleum. Though of course

21

they didn't dare laugh, Mom and Alvin smirked a little.

"Are you okay, Dad?" Alvin asked, trying hard not to giggle.

"Just great," Dad said crabbily, rubbing his behind. "Wonderful. Groovy. Never better."

"Look!" cried Annie, a bit too late to do any good. "There's one I missed!" She picked up the stray toothpick and handed it to her father. He thanked her politely, but for some reason or other she got the feeling he was definitely in a grumpy mood.

3

"I'll drive," said Mom. She thought Dad ought to take it easy for a while after his fall.

"I'll navigate," Alvin offered. "Let me ride up front."

"Why not?" said Dad, and he climbed into the backseat with Annie.

When they all finished belting themselves in, Mom started the engine. Just then Annie hollered, "Where's Lambie?"

Everybody looked. He wasn't on the floor, he wasn't under the seat, he wasn't on the back ledge, and he wasn't in the glove compartment. Alvin wasn't sitting on him, and neither was anybody else. Annie began to cry. "He's gone!" she sobbed. "Lambie's gone!"

"We'll find him," Dad said.

"No, you won't. He's gone!"

"He didn't just walk away," Alvin helpfully pointed out.

"Yes, he did," Annie moaned. "He was my best friend, and he just walked away. He'll never come back."

Alvin was about to argue the point, when the hostess rushed out of the coffee shop, waving Lambie frantically in the air. "Good thing I found you! You left this behind!" she told Alvin, handing the plush pet to him through the window.

"That's my sister's," he replied, trying to make sure the woman understood he was too old for fluffy toys.

"Gimme!" cried Annie, and Alvin did. She hugged and kissed her tiny friend so hard his eyes bulged out.

"Thank you so much," Mom told the hostess. "I don't know what we'd've done without Lambie."

"I can just imagine! My littlest has a bullfrog named Clancy. Half the time she goes around the house croaking."

Dad reminded Annie to thank the hostess, and Annie stopped fluffing Lambie's fur and primping his blue ribbon just long enough to do it. Then Mom put the car in gear, Alvin gave her directions, and off they went.

They were well past the Muckleburg city limits when Annie put Lambie aside for a while. "What are we going to do with all those toothpicks?" she asked.

"You can play pickup sticks," Dad suggested.

"We just did that," Annie frowned, "and it wasn't much fun."

"It's a game," Alvin explained. "You throw the sticks on a table, and then you try to pick them up one at a time without moving the others."

"That sounds dumb," Annie said.

"Alvin could build a toothpick castle," Mom suggested.

"Sure," agreed Alvin. "I could glue them together and make all sorts of things."

"Could you make a house for Lambie?"

"If I wanted to."

"Hear that, Lambie? Alvin's gonna build you a house!" Lambie was so delighted, he bounced up and down with a little of Annie's help. "Lambie loves you," she told Alvin. He wasn't sure just how she could tell, but he was pleased all the same.

"You know what else we could do?" he said. "We could plant toothpicks in the backyard. Then they'd grow into a toothpick tree."

"What's a toothpick tree?"

Alvin put his imagination into high gear. "It's a big, tall tree with a very skinny trunk and no bark at all, and in the fall you get toothpicks from it."

"Sounds like quite a useful plant," Dad said, chuckling.

"Is that where toothpicks come from?" Annie asked.

"Absolutely," said Alvin. "The round ones come from round toothpick trees, and the flat ones come from flat toothpick trees. And the plastic ones . . ."

"Don't tell me," Mom interrupted. "Let me guess."

"Surely you've heard of Johnny Toothpickseed," Dad reminded everybody. "He walked all across the country with a bag of toothpicks on his back and planted them everywhere he went."

"Enough, already!" said Mom.

"When we get home, can I grow a toothpick tree?" Annie asked.

"You can try," Mom sighed.

"Oh, boy!" said Alvin. "Then in the fall we can bake fresh toothpick pies!"

The morning was beginning to get warm, but a pleasant breeze swept through the Hooples' car as it sped along the highway. "Knee high by the Fourth of July," Dad remarked as they approached a green field of corn, even though it was already the middle of August and the stalks were taller than he was. No matter what the time of year or the height of the stalks, Dad always said, "Knee high by the Fourth of July" whenever he spotted a cornfield, because that was what *his* dad had told him the farmers always said. Alvin had heard it before. Often.

"That line's getting pretty corny," he said.

"Meet old Pop Corn himself," Mom teased. "He's got a million of 'em."

"I'll say," said Alvin, watching the field pass by. "Hey, look! Cows!"

"Look, Lambie!" said Annie excitedly, holding him up to the window for a better view.

"That's where our milk comes from," Dad explained.

"Which one?" Annie asked.

"Which one what?" asked Dad.

"Which one of those cows gives us our milk?"

"All of them. The farmers take the milk from all the cows and mix it together in big vats before they pasteurize it and sell it to us."

"Except the brown cows. They give chocolate milk," Alvin kidded.

26

"And you say *I* tell corny jokes!" Dad complained.

"Alvin, you shouldn't tease your sister all the time. She'll get the wrong idea," Mom scolded. Alvin just grinned.

"What flavor do the black cows give?" Annie asked.

"Don't say a word," Mom warned Alvin. Alvin kept his mouth shut.

"Well?" demanded Annie. "What flavor?"

Even though Mom was waggling her finger at him, Alvin just couldn't resist. "Licorice," he whispered.

"But I didn't see any white cows," Annie realized. "Where are all the cows that give white milk?"

"Okay, wise guy," Dad said to Alvin. "Let's see you answer that one."

Alvin thought for a moment. "They're in the barn," he said finally.

"Why?" asked Annie.

Alvin was afraid she'd ask that. He thought some more. "Because if they go outside in the summertime, they get all sunburned and red, and then they give strawberry milk."

"Holy cow!" Dad said, shaking his head.

"I want some strawberry milk," Annie declared.

Annie could make herself a real nuisance when she got an idea like that in her head, so Dad tried to think of a way to change the subject. She saved him the trouble. "Yuck!" she exclaimed, pointing at a herd of hairless creatures in a nearby meadow. "What kind of animals are those?"

"Sheep," said Mom.

"But sheeps are fuzzy. Like Lambie."

"Sheep are usually woolly," Dad explained, "except when the farmers shear them, which is what must've happened to those fellows over there."

"Bet they don't like it much," said Annie.

"Aw, it's just like getting a haircut," Alvin scoffed.

"How do *you* know, Mr. Smarty?" Annie whined. "You're not a sheep."

"No," Alvin roared. "I'm a wolf!" And with a fearsome growl, he turned around and snatched Lambie right out of Annie's hands.

"Give him back!" Annie screamed.

"Grrrr! I'm gonna eat him up!" Alvin growled.

"Give me back my Lambie!"

Alvin just growled louder and pawed at Lambie's coat. "Come on, Alvin," Mom pleaded. "Give him back. We've had enough trouble with Lambie today."

Alvin growled some more and pretended to take a bite out of Lambie's foot. Annie shrieked so loud Mom nearly drove off the road.

"Alvin . . ." Dad said sternly. "Give him back. One . . . two . . ."

Alvin knew he'd be in for it if Dad got to three. He tossed Lambie back to Annie.

She straightened Lambie's ribbon and hugged him tight. "I love you better than all those big old sheeps put together," she said. "You're more fluffier." Then she stuck her tongue out at Alvin and told him Lambie didn't love him anymore. Alvin said that was fine with him and growled back as if he were thinking of snatching Lambie again. Annie clutched her plush pal even tighter.

"Peace!" Mom exclaimed. "It's song time!" She began to sing "On Top of Old Smoky," and Dad joined in. Alvin would much rather have continued pestering Annie, but when your parents are singing "On Top of Old Smoky" at the top of their lungs, there's not much else you can do but sing along. So everybody sang "The Bear Went over the Mountain," and "Yo Ho Ho and a Bottle of Rum," and "Buffalo Gals," and "John Jacob Jingleheimer Schmitt," and "Yellow Submarine," and "Blowin' in the Wind," and a lot of other stuff. Annie went "lalalalala" quite a bit because she didn't know all the words, but nobody really minded.

They stopped singing for a while when Dad noticed that the mileage counter—he called it the "odometer"—in the middle of the speedometer was reading 29999.8. It changed to 29999.9, and then all the numbers rolled up at the same time and it read 30000.0. Everybody except Annie was very impressed. Then they all started to sing "A Hundred Bottles of Beer on the Wall," but there were still forty-two bottles left when Mom announced it was lunchtime.

The highway outside the town of Bugler was swarming with restaurants. A dozen big tractor-trailers were parked outside the Truck Stop Café, which claimed it had "CB Chow," whatever that might be. The Friendly Diner looked like a rusty train car and advertised "Home-Cooked Vittles at Popular Prices." And Alvin kept a watchful eye on The Leaning Tower of Pizza; it looked as though it might topple over any minute and drop a load of pepperoni on the road. But Mrs. Hoople knew what her kids liked best, so she pulled over at the sign of the enormous walking hamburger munching on a whole family of hungry travelers. Monsterburgers were Alvin's special favorites.

"Nothing like a good dose of junk food to perk you right up," said Dad. He and Alvin picked up their order at a little window in front and joined Mom and Annie at a picnic bench around the side. As they started to eat, a sociable sparrow flew up and did a little dance for them.

"I wonder if he's hungry," said Mom, breaking off a hunk of her Spookburger bun and holding it out to him. The sparrow chirped happily and ate it right from her hand.

"That is one clever bird," said Dad between mouthfuls of the triple Dracuburger he'd ordered after deciding he deserved a lunch break from his diet. He held out part of his bun, and the sparrow hopped over to him and pecked away at it delightedly.

Alvin wanted the sparrow to eat from his hand, but he was too hungry to consider offering him even a tiny morsel of his double-cheese Frankenburger, so he held out a piece of its greasy paper wrapper instead. Somebody else must've tried that trick on the sparrow before. He shook his head, scolded Alvin, and hopped over to Annie. She offered him a French fry and squealed with joy when he picked it up. He flew it to the roof of the Hooples' car and nibbled on it happily.

"He must really love French fries," Alvin mumbled with his mouth full.

"I guess we have a friend for life," said Mom.

Their new-found chum left a white puddle on the

windshield and flew away. "Well, that's gratitude for you!" Dad said, shaking his head. "I thought he'd give us a little serenade."

There's no way to be dainty when you eat a Monsterburger. When everybody had finished wiping ketchup and mustard and relish and Monster Sauce from lips and chins and noses, Dad led them all to the little window to get some ice cream. Mom and Alvin ordered large chocolate cones. Annie's mind was still on those sunburned cows, so she asked for a small strawberry. Unfortunately, they were out of that flavor, and she had to settle for vanilla. Dad thought he'd better get back on his diet. He didn't order anything.

Mom had to wipe some leftover mustard from Annie's forehead, so she asked Dad to hold her cone for a second. But when she took it back, it was just a tiny stub with no ice cream in it at all. Mom scowled. "I asked you to hold it, not eat it."

"Sorry," Dad apologized, a little embarrassed. "I couldn't resist." He bought Mom another cone to make up for it. Then he decided he might just as well forget about his diet till dinnertime, and he ordered a cone of his own. "Just a medium one, though," he told the girl behind the window. "No sense overdoing it."

"Right, Dad," Alvin agreed. "How about another one for me, too? Just a medium one. No sense overdoing it."

4

"Yow!" Alvin shouted as he sat down in the car. "This seat's hot enough to melt my rear end off!"

"Oh, it's not so bad," said Dad, licking his cone as he sat down in the back with Annie. "It'll cool off fast enough once we get on the road."

Mom slid behind the wheel, and everybody got belted in. Mom was all ready to start the engine when she heard something funny.

"What's that buzzing?" she asked.

"I don't hear anything," Dad said.

"Me neither," said Annie.

Then Alvin saw the troublemaker: a huge yellow bumblebee hovering beside Mom's ear. "Don't move, Mom," Alvin advised her. "It's a bee."

"Where?" she asked, slightly upset. Bees were not her favorite insects.

"It was right by your ear, but it just flew toward Annie," Alvin said.

"Go away, bee!" Annie yelled, waving her arms all over the place to shoo him away.

"Keep still," Dad said. "If you don't bother him, he'll probably just fly away."

The bee buzzed around Annie for a while. Then it flew under Dad's nose. Then it landed on Lambie's forehead. But Annie wasn't about to let her best friend get stung. She slapped her little hand right down on top of the bee and squooshed him into Lambie's fur. "That's the end of *that* bee," she said, calmly flicking his remains out of Lambie's coat.

"Boy, was that dumb," Alvin said. "You're lucky you didn't get stung."

"Lambie doesn't like bees," Annie declared, "and I don't either."

"Bees don't usually do you any harm," Dad said. "Please try not to squash them anymore."

"We'll squash 'em all!" Annie boasted. "We don't like bees!"

There was no use arguing with Annie when she got into one of her stubborn moods. "Is everybody set?" Mom asked.

Everybody was. She started the engine and pulled out onto the highway.

"How about a little music?" Dad asked.

"Great idea!" said Alvin. He turned on the radio and pushed the button for his favorite station, but all he got was crackly static.

"You'll have to use the knob now," Dad said. "We're too far away to get the stations from home."

Alvin twiddled the dial. A snappy jingle hit him in the ears:

If you're looking for a car,
Get all the facts,
Then drive right in
To see Crazy Max.

If you're ready to give
Your old jalopy the axe,
Then you should be talking
To that goofball Max.

If oomph is what your car now lacks,
If it squeaks and rattles and clatters and clacks,
If it guzzles gas, eats between-pump snacks,
Trade it in on a creampuff from Madman Max.

Max
Max
Max
Max
On Highway 21 in Wilmerdale.

That was all Max had to say for himself. Horace
Hackenback of Hackenback's Food City started to
announce low, low prices on casaba melons, and Alvin twirled the knob. He found a Beatles oldie that
Mom and Dad wanted to hear, but it kept fading in
and out and getting fuzzy. Alvin thought it sounded
awfully mushy anyhow, so he turned the knob farther
and found the end of the current number-one hit tune.
He and Annie had heard it so many times they knew
all the words, and they started to sing along. But before the song was over, a loony voice broke in and

screamed, "Waaaaaaaal, all *right!* This is T.J., your deejay, comin' at you live on fifty-five, WWWP, woo-woo-woo-POW! Hot and happy in happenin' Zieglerville."

"Why don't you change the station?" asked Mom. But Alvin sort of liked T.J. the Deejay. He turned up the volume instead.

"Temperature right smack dab in the heart of sizzling downtown Zieglerville? A scorching ninety-one degrees and going, up, *up, UP!* Hot enough for you? Why, it's so hot in here, that last record just melted into a little black puddle on my turntable. Heck, a minute ago I took a couple of ice cubes out of the freezer, and you know what? They jumped back in!"

"Boy, it sure is hot," said Annie.

"Lemme tell you," T.J. went on, "it's so hot to-day, the corn's popping right off the ears."

Annie checked the cornfields. "I don't see any ears popping."

"*My* ears are popping," said Mom.

" . . . And that's not all," T.J. continued. "It's such a scorcher, the cows are giving melted but-ter!"

"I want some popcorn," Annie declared.

"*Please* change the station," Mom begged.

Alvin reluctantly turned the dial. He found a slow, syrupy ballad and was reaching for the knob again when Dad said, "Hold on! That's an Elvis song!"

"They just don't write 'em like that anymore," Mom sighed.

35

"I'm sure glad of that," said Alvin.

"Are we there yet?" Annie whined. Sooner or later Annie always got bored and cranky when the family went for a long drive. Alvin thought he might be able to entertain her, so he turned off the radio and gave it a try.

"Look, Annie! See that puddle of water up ahead?"

"Where?" she asked as it disappeared from view.

"You missed it," said Alvin, looking for another one. "Up there on the road! See it?"

Annie looked hard. "I think so."

"Watch what happens when we get closer."

Annie did. Just as they neared it, the shimmering patch of water disappeared, and the road was dry. "Where'd it go?" she wondered.

"Here comes another one," said Dad. "Look closer."

Annie leaned forward and stared at the glistening spot. All of a sudden it disappeared just like the first one. "We must be scaring it away!" she cried.

"No, Annie. It's a mirage," Alvin explained.

"Huh?"

"There really isn't any water at all. It only looks that way."

"But there's water over *there.*" She pointed to a sprinkler spraying crops in a field. "So *that* must be water, too." She pointed to another shiny spot in the road ahead.

"But it isn't. It's an optical illusion."

"I don't get it."

"When the light and the air are just right, you see the sky reflected in the road," Dad explained. "It only looks like there's water there."

36

"But *that's* water," said Annie, pointing ahead.

"No," said Alvin without even looking. "It's another mirage."

"It sure looks like water."

"It'll disappear just like all the others."

"Bet it won't."

"Bet it will."

"Will not."

"Will too."

"Will not!"

"Will too!"

Splash! The Hooples' car whizzed through a little stream trickling across the road from a dripping pipe. "You can't fool me," Annie gloated triumphantly. "I'll bet you can't build houses out of toothpicks, either." Lambie agreed, so she gave him a big kiss. Alvin just shook his head.

Annie was bored with disappearing puddles anyhow. "I'm going to count my mosquito bites," she announced. "One . . . two . . . three . . ."

She thought and thought, but she couldn't remember what was next. "What comes after three?" she asked.

"Four," Alvin sneered.

"It does not, liar," Annie whined back.

Alvin sighed. Sometimes little sisters can be big pains.

5

"Lambie has to go to the bathroom," Annie announced a few miles later.

"Is Lambie sure about that?" Mom asked.

"Positive."

Everybody kept an eye out for a gas station or a rest area, but public toilets were scarce as strawberry milk on this stretch of road. Alvin checked the map and learned that the next town was only five miles away, but Lambie's friend insisted he couldn't wait that long.

Wait he did, though, until a cozy little filling station with a "Clean Rest Rooms" sign came into view. Mom pulled up to the pumps.

"Fill 'er up?" asked the attendant, a long-haired high-school kid who seemed eager to help.

Mom nodded. "Regular, please. Where are your rest rooms?"

"To the right of the building, there. You can't miss 'em."

Mom and Annie and Lambie went off to the ladies' room, and Alvin to the men's. For some reason, Dad hardly ever had to go to the bathroom when they went

38

on trips, so he stayed behind and watched the attendant clean the windows and check the oil.

Except for a few pesky flies who seemed to resent a human's intrusion, Alvin thought the bathroom was almost as clean as advertised. But he was disappointed it didn't have one of those sanitary electric hand dryers, especially when he discovered that the towel holder was empty.

As he stepped outside, Mom caught him wiping his wet hands on his pants. "Alvin, those are your newest jeans," she scolded.

"But they're all out of towels," he explained. Even so, Mom insisted, there must be a better way for him to dry his hands. But she never did tell him what it might be.

"I need a candy bar," Annie declared, pointing to an inviting vending machine.

"It's too soon after lunch," Mom replied.

"Boy! You're no fun!" Annie griped. Mom just frowned back.

When they got to the car, Dad was signing the credit-card slip. He'd opened all the car doors wide, so it wouldn't get too hot inside. "Mind if I ride up front with my sweetie, otherwise known as your mother, for a while?" he asked Alvin.

"Yes, I mind," Alvin replied. He liked riding up front with the driver, and he didn't feel like sitting in back with Annie again, especially now that she was getting cranky.

"But it *is* my turn," Dad said.

"No, it isn't," Annie grumbled. "It's *my* turn."

"I think you'd better stay in the back," Mom said.

"We've still got quite a way to go, and you might want to take a nap."

"No, I won't," said Annie.

"Alvin and Annie!" Dad ordered cheerfully. "Backseat!" They climbed in and fastened their seat belts.

Dad had pretty much recovered from his fall, so he decided to drive again. Alvin checked his maps even though he wasn't in the official navigator's seat. "Keep your eyes open for the Interstate Highway," he said. "It should be coming up very soon."

Sure enough, a few minutes later, Dad turned onto a wide superhighway where everybody seemed to be speeding. There were two lanes in each direction, and big trucks whizzing by, and no houses or shops or restaurants by the side of the road. Mom and Dad said the scenery was beautiful. Alvin thought it was kind of lonely and boring, and wished they were on a road where you could see billboards and Yummy-Freezes and Wienie Kings and golden arches and barns with cows and horses. But Dad explained they'd make a lot better time on the Interstate, and that satisfied Alvin. He wanted to get to the Philadelphia ball park early so he could watch batting practice.

Annie really needed a nap. She was getting extremely irritable. Twice in half a minute, she whined "Are we there yet?" When she asked a third time, Mom suggested she lie down for a while. But Annie didn't want to do any such thing. She started punching Alvin instead.

"Cut it out!" Alvin yelled, and punched her right back.

"Ow! Alvin punched me!" Annie cried.

"She punched me first," her brother pointed out.

"Alvin, you're not supposed to punch your sister," Mom told him.

"She's not supposed to punch me, either," Alvin protested.

"True," Dad admitted. "Annie, why don't you take a nap?"

"Don't want to."

"Well, please don't punch Alvin anymore."

"Okay." Annie sat still for at least eleven seconds, and then she started kicking the back of Mom's seat.

"Annie, please stop kicking my seat," Mom said.

"I wasn't."

"Well, somebody was, and I don't think it was Lambie."

Annie suddenly looked worried. She rummaged through the pile of stuff on the seat, and she looked worrieder. "Lambie! Where's my Lambie?"

Dad had to keep his eyes on the road, but everybody else searched through the car. Lambie was nowhere to be found. Annie started to cry.

Alvin smirked. "Serves you right. Maybe he got mad because you punched me."

"I didn't mean to punch you," Annie sobbed. "I want my Lambie!"

"When did you last have him with you?" Dad asked.

"Just now," Annie said.

"I'll bet Lambie's back there at the gas station," Mom said in an exasperated tone.

"Turn around!" Annie cried.

"I can't just turn around on this road," Dad explained patiently. "We have to get off the road and then get back on again."

"Well, do it, then!" Annie wailed.

"The very first chance we get," said Dad.

"But that might make us late for the game!" Alvin shouted.

"Oh, we should still get there on time," Dad said.

"But I wanted to be real early! What if they run out of bats?"

"I want my Lambie!" Annie screamed.

"You and your stupid Lambie!" Alvin shouted. "Why can't you take better care of him?"

"You shut up, Alvin. Lambie hates you."

"I hate him, too."

At the next exit, Dad drove the car off the superhighway, across an overpass, and back onto the highway again in the other direction. Alvin sulked. He wondered if they'd ever get to Philadelphia. His seatmate wasn't very cheerful, either. She'd stopped crying once Dad had turned the car around, but every now and then she'd sob a little and say "Lambie!" in a pitiful voice.

Mom and Dad tried to cheer everybody up by singing, but Annie spoiled the songs by screaming, "Stop it, stop it, stop it!" over and over. Dad finally turned on the radio, and everybody listened to lots and lots of commercials and the occasional songs that interrupted them. Every chance she got, Annie would say, "I want my Lambie," and Alvin would scowl at her, and Mom and Dad would tell her they were almost there.

Finally they turned off the superhighway and

passed ice-cream stands and used-car lots and restaurants. In a few minutes they were back at the gas station where they'd stopped before. Mom and Annie got out and searched the ladies' room. Lambie wasn't there.

They went into the office. "Excuse me," Mom asked a man in coveralls who was recording a sale on the credit-card machine. "Did anyone happen to find a little lamb in the ladies' room?"

"You took a sheep to the ladies' room?" asked the amazed attendant.

"My daughter's. A toy one."

The man looked relieved. "I haven't seen one. Check with Joe over there." He pointed to a pair of legs sticking out from under a car in the garage.

By this time Dad and Alvin were wondering what was going on. They joined Mom and Annie in the garage just as the pair of legs, with a greasy mechanic attached, slid out from under the car. "Excuse me," Mom said. "Did anyone find a little toy sheep in the ladies' room?"

"It was my Lambie," Annie explained.

The repairman frowned. He put down his wrench and wiped his oily hands on his pants. "At least *my* hands were clean," thought Alvin, hoping Mom noticed.

The mechanic walked over to a big can marked "Rags." He reached in and pulled out a Lambie-shaped object dripping with greasy black oil. "This it?" he asked.

Out of the soggy black mess stared two dirty blue eyes Annie would have recognized anywhere. "Lambie!" she cried, and ran toward him.

43

"Thought he was one of our oil rags," said the mechanic apologetically.

"He's no oil rag! He's my Lambie! Give him to me!" Annie shouted. The man was just about to oblige her when Mom asked him not to. She stooped down to talk with her daughter.

"Honey," Mom said soothingly, "he's not much of a toy anymore. I don't think we could ever get him clean."

"I don't care," said Annie. "I want my Lambie."

"He'd just get oil all over you and everything he touched. We'll find you another Lambie."

"But he's my friend. He loves me."

Dad picked Annie up and hugged her. "We do, too, you know."

"But that's different. I want my Lambie."

Alvin folded his arms across his chest and tapped his foot. He was getting very impatient.

Dad ignored him. "I realize you're disappointed," he told Annie. "But you wouldn't want a pet who got you and your friends all dirty every time you touched him."

"Yes, I would," Annie pouted.

"Don't you think it'd be better if we let him stay here and help this man fix people's cars?"

"No."

"I bet he'd be very good at it."

"But . . ."

"Come on, Annie. Let's let Lambie do his work."

"But . . ."

"Say good-bye to him."

"But . . ."

"Come on, now."

44

"Good-bye, Lambie," Annie sniffled.

Dad brushed away her tears. "Would a candy bar help cheer you up?" he asked.

"No," Annie snuffled. "Maybe some strawberry ice cream . . ."

"Done!" Dad boomed, and carried her to the car.

Mom thanked the mechanic for his help, and he made sure Annie wasn't looking when he tossed Lambie back into the rag bin.

Everybody got into the car and rolled down the highway to the Yummy-Freeze stand. Mom and Alvin and poor defenseless Dad all had big gooey sundaes in plastic boats, and Annie liked her strawberry ice cream so much she forgot all about Lambie for a while. But when they got back in the car and started down the road, Annie began to sob.

"What's the matter?" Alvin asked.

"I miss my Lambie," Annie whimpered.

"I'll bet he misses you, too," said Alvin, trying to cheer her up. "But you know, just the other day, he told me that more than anything else in the world, the one thing he really wanted to be was an auto mechanic."

"Really?"

"Really. In a gas station just like the one where he's working."

"Alvin, that's a lie," Annie sobbed. "He told me he wanted to be the chef at Chick's Chicken Kitchen. And I want him back!"

Mom looked at Dad.

"I don't care if he is filthy!"

Dad looked at Mom.

"I want my Lambie back!" Annie wailed. Mom

turned around to look at her, and Dad glanced at her in the rearview mirror. Then Dad gave Mom a funny look, let out a big sigh, and turned the car around.

"Are we going back for Lambie?" Annie asked.

"That's exactly what we're doing," Dad replied.

Annie's face lit up. Alvin wanted to tell her that if she kept smiling so wide, her teeth would fall out, but he realized she wasn't in the mood for teasing just now. And neither was he. It was getting later and later, but instead of speeding toward Philadelphia, they were heading in exactly the opposite direction. "What about the ball game?" Alvin demanded.

"We still have plenty of time," Dad said.

"I sure hope so," Alvin grumbled. "It'd sure be a shame to miss a once-in-a-lifetime opportunity because of some stupid stuffed toy."

"He's not stupid! He's my Lambie!" Annie cried, and punched Alvin in the arm. Alvin seriously thought about punching her back, but he put on his fielder's glove and punched that instead.

When they got back to the gas station, Mom told everybody else to stay put. She hopped out, opened the trunk, took a clear plastic bag from one of the suitcases, and went into the garage.

From the car, Annie and Alvin could see the mechanic shuffle over to the rag bin and dig out Annie's filthy friend. Mom held the plastic bag open wide, and the man dropped Lambie in. Then Mom came back to the car.

"Gimme!" Annie demanded, reaching so hard toward Lambie that her arm hurt.

"Let's get one thing straight first, little shepherd," Mom said as she sealed the bag with some ad-

46

hesive tape from the first-aid kit. "I won't be able to get Lambie cleaned up till we get home, if I can get him clean at all. In the meantime, we'll keep him wrapped up in this plastic bag. You can see him, he can see you, and the grease will stay inside. You can cuddle him and play with him as much as you want, as long as you don't open the bag. But the minute you do, that'll be the last you see of Lambie for quite some time. Do you understand?"

"Yes," said Annie in a very quiet voice. "Now may I please have my Lambie?"

Mom handed him to her. "Boy, he's a mess," said Alvin.

"I'll say," Annie agreed, hugging the bag hard. "He's not much fun like this."

"You'll just have to make do till we get back home," said Mom.

"Can he hear me in there?" Annie asked.

"Perfectly," said Dad.

Annie shouted anyhow, just to make sure. "I love you, Lambie! Let's take a nap now!"

She hugged the plastic bag tight in her arms, stretched out on the seat, and dozed off. Alvin wished she wouldn't kick so much. But at least she was asleep, and the car was pointed toward Philadelphia.

Nothing would stop them now!

6

The superhighway was even more boring the second time around, since everybody had to be quiet so as not to waken Annie. Alvin riffled through his baseball cards to make sure they were all in order, but when he started to feel a little carsick from reading the backs, he thought he'd better put them aside.

He checked out his lightning bugs. They looked kind of lethargic. Maybe the heat was slowing them down. Alvin tapped on the jar, and a couple of the fireflies moved, but he couldn't tell for sure whether they were crawling or just sliding along the glass. Lightning bugs, Alvin knew well, tend to die on you all of a sudden. One of his great ambitions was to collect a jarful of fireflies as bright as a flashlight, but he never could keep enough of them alive at once to make it work.

He put down the jar. He really didn't want to admit it, but he was getting drowsy. Even though a lot of air blew through the car, the heat and humidity kept getting worse and worse as the day wore on. When Dad pulled out to pass an ice cream truck, Alvin could almost taste the frozen malt bar painted on the back.

He checked his maps. There was still a long way to go before they'd be in Philadelphia. He was trying to figure out exactly how far, and how long it would take, when a carful of high-school kids passed his window. The driver was honking his horn, and the others were pointing and hollering at the Hooples. "These kids today are even worse than we were!" Dad laughed as they passed. But then an old lady and man in a passing station wagon honked and pointed, too, and Alvin noticed something peculiar on Dad's instrument panel.

"Your red light that says 'TEMP' is on," he said.

"Uh-oh," Dad worried, taking a look for himself.

"Are we overheating?" Mom asked.

"Looks that way," Dad replied. He slowed down and pulled over to the side of the road. The car bounced to a stop.

"Are we there yet?" Annie asked, waking up.

Whoosh! Before anybody had time to answer her, thick white billows of steam rose from beneath the hood. "Wow!" said Annie. "I guess we aren't, huh?" She and Alvin had never seen anything like it.

Dad and Mom helped them get out of the car on the side away from the road. Everybody stood and watched as the big white clouds kept puffing up from under the hood. Some steam even rose from beneath the passenger compartment.

"I guess that's what all those people were honking about," Mom said to Dad. "How come you didn't notice the light?"

"Beats me," said Dad, scratching his head.

Mom sighed. "Well, it's a good thing Alvin's got such sharp eyes, or we might be in worse shape."

49

Alvin beamed. "You're welcome. Now let's fix it."

Dad frowned. "I don't think we can."

"But we have to get to the game!" Alvin moaned. "What do we do now?"

"A very good question," said Dad. "What we do is put up our hood, once it's cool enough to handle. Then we tie a handkerchief to our radio antenna and wait till somebody notices it and stops to help us."

Unfortunately, nobody had a handkerchief, and Kleenex wasn't strong enough to hold. Alvin offered to donate a pair of his underpants to the cause, but once Dad got the hood up, he didn't think the white flag would be necessary.

They waited a good long while by the roadside. Summer bugs flitted around their heads and feasted on their arms and necks. A big dragonfly scared Annie. Everybody got hot and sweaty and crabby, and it seemed as if none of the passing cars would ever stop to lend a hand.

At first Alvin thought this was really quite an adventure, but soon he got as grumpy as everyone else. Grumpier, even, because he began to picture himself stuck out here in the middle of nowhere scratching his insect bites while thousands of happy kids in Philadelphia were admiring their bats. Just when he'd begun to give up hope, a big tractor-trailer pulled over and parked a few yards ahead. A big, wide, friendly-looking woman in blue jeans and a checkered blouse got out and walked up to them. "Howdy, folks! Boiled over?"

"That's about the size of it," Dad said.

"Well, I ought to be able to rustle up some help on

my CB. Maybe your kids'd like to see the rig while I'm at it.''

"I wouldn't mind seeing it myself," Mom said.

"Well, come on, then," said the woman. She said her name was Sadie McGlinn, and she shook hands with the entire Hoople family except Lambie. Then she helped Annie and Alvin up to the cab of her truck.

The inside looked the way Alvin had always imagined a spaceship would. A dazzling instrument panel full of lights and dials and meters curved all around the tall driver's seat, which was nearly as comfortable as the chairs in the Hooples' living room. Sadie turned on the tape machine and played one of Alvin's favorite tunes. She told Annie to push a little button, and a blast from the air horn deafened everybody. Best of all, the cab was cool and comfortable. "Boy!" said Alvin, taking in the view of the highway down below. "This is the way to travel."

"It's neat," said Annie as Mom and Dad peeked in.

"You bet your booties, grandma," said Sadie as she grabbed her CB microphone. "Breaker nine, breaker nine. Breaker nine, breaker nine. Lazy Susan here."

Nobody answered. "Breaker nine, breaker nine. Come on, out there! Lazy Susan needs some help."

"Come on, Lazy Susan," the radio squawked. "Ace high with ears on."

' "Got a radiator blew its stack out here at post one four seven. They're looking for assistance."

"Uh, roger, Lazy Sue. One four seven. We'll get a man out there as soon as we can. Eights and other good ones to you."

51

"Same to you, good buddy, and thank you kindly. We gone!" said Sadie. She put the handset back on the hook.

"I wish we had one of those," Alvin said.

"Comes in right handy in a jam," said Sadie, turning to Dad. "Somebody ought to be along real soon." Then she helped Annie and Alvin down from the cab and back out into the sweltering outdoor air.

Mom and Dad thanked Ms. McGlinn for everything she'd done. "Just doing my bit," she said. "Now, if you really want to thank me, just slide right on over next time one of us eighteen-wheelers comes up behind you and gives you a toot."

"We sure will," Dad replied. Sadie climbed up to the cab of her truck. As she drove away, the Hooples waved good-bye. Sadie gave them an earpiercing blast on her horn and waved back.

"That's what I want to do when I get big," said Annie.

"Well, I want to be a baseball player," Alvin declared, "and you can't do that unless you show up at the game."

"Relax," Dad said. "Maybe they'll be able to fix us right up. We could still make it."

"I sure hope so," Alvin grumbled.

A few hundred mosquito bites later, a wrecking truck from Slim's Super Service Station drove up. Out jumped a big sweaty fellow in a dirty gray gas-station uniform. An embroidered patch over his heart said "Marlin."

"Looks like the heat was too much for her," he said with a smile as he squeezed one of the hoses under the hood. "Start'er up."

Mr. Hoople got into the car and turned the key. The engine started, but after a second or two it coughed, sputtered, and died.

Marlin grinned. "Feels like your thermostat's stuck shut."

"Can you fix it?" Dad asked, frowning. Alvin frowned, too. At the moment, he didn't think there was much to grin about.

"Have to tow her in," Marlin said.

"How long will it take?" Mom asked.

"To fix? Depends. Don't know if we have the right part for a foreign job like this one. If we do, you're out in two shakes of a lamb's tail," Marlin explained. Annie smiled and shook Lambie's bag up and down.

"What if you don't have the part?" Alvin asked.

"Then you're out of luck till tomorrow morning at the earliest."

"Oh, boy," said Dad dejectedly. "Where's your garage?"

"In Appleton. About ten miles up the road."

"Is there a motel in town if we have to stay the night?" Mom asked.

"Two of 'em. You can have your pick."

"But we have to get to Philadelphia tonight!" Alvin shouted. "We can't just stay out here!"

Marlin beamed. "If we have that part of yours, maybe you won't have to."

Alvin just scowled.

Marlin got back inside his tow truck and pushed forward on a lever. A winch in back slowly lowered a cable with a big hook on the end. Marlin got out of the truck and fastened the hook underneath the Hooples' car. Then he went back in and pulled on the lever. The winch wound the cable up again, and the front of the Hooples' car magically rose into the air.

Alvin was still worried about missing Bat Night, but he had to admit he never expected to see anything like this on his vacation. "Do we have to sit in the car?" he asked, secretly hoping he'd be able to ride up front in the wrecker.

"Wouldn't be safe," said the mechanic. "You'll all have to squeeze in the cab with me."

Mom and Dad got in first. Alvin sat on Dad's lap, Annie squirmed around on Mom's, and away they went, dragging their car behind them. The hot, dirty cab of the tow truck was kind of disappointing after Sadie's fancy machine, but compared to a lot of things people do on their vacations, Alvin thought, this was pretty exciting.

It was especially neat when Marlin finished radioing his position to the garage. He handed Alvin the microphone and told him to push the button and say, "A big ten four to you, pardner." Alvin did just that, and he was tickled when the radio squawked back, "Same to you, big fella."

The sign at the city limits said "Welcome to Appleton. Speed Limit 25. Radar Enforced. Eat More Apples." A minute later, the tow truck turned in at Slim's Super Service Station. Everybody got out, and Marlin lowered the car. Dad thought he did it a little too fast, since the car bounced three or four times when it hit the ground, but Marlin assured him there was no harm done.

Everybody stood around impatiently while Marlin checked to see whether he had the part he needed to fix the car. He didn't. He couldn't do anything with the car till morning.

Alvin got an awful feeling in his stomach. "What about the game?" he shouted. "What about my bat?"

"We're sorry, Alvin," Mom said.

"We know how disappointed you are," said Dad.

"This is the worst thing that's ever happened to me!" Alvin groaned.

"I'm sorry," Dad said. "It couldn't be helped."

"But how am I going to get my bat now?" Alvin wailed.

"We'll figure something out," Dad said. "I'm not any too happy about being stuck in Appleton for the night myself."

"Oh, that's not such a terrible fate," said a fat, jolly, gray-haired man in coveralls who turned out to be Slim himself, the garage's owner and Marlin's father. "We've got a bustling little community here and a fine and dandy motel just the other side of town. I'd be glad to give you a lift over there." So Mom and Dad and Alvin and Annie toted their luggage and Lambie to Slim's station wagon, and he drove them down Appleton's main street.

It was a lot bigger than Alvin had expected. He noticed two drugstores, a movie theater, a pet shop, a five-and-ten, a hardware store, a fried-chicken place, and quite a few other little shops. But it didn't have the Liberty Bell or Independence Hall or the Mint, and it didn't have Veterans Stadium, where the Phillies played, or Bat Night, either. Alvin tried very hard to keep from crying.

7

The car turned a corner. Slim pointed to a long, low building up ahead, and when they got closer, Alvin could read the sign: "FINE AND DANDY MOTEL." Slim parked in front of the office, and everybody went in. The frosty air conditioning made Alvin feel a little better.

"Do you have any rooms for tonight?" Dad asked the sour-faced man behind the desk.

"Rooms?" the crotchety manager asked back, keeping one eye on Annie to make sure she didn't try to play with the little china apples next to the postcard rack. "Plenty of 'em. Any one you want, except number twelve, 'cause that one's mine. How about number three? It's got a double bed and two rollaways all set up."

When Mom left to take a look at the room, Alvin noticed a Phillies schedule posted beside the office door. It was there just to torment him, Alvin thought. As if flashing in neon, two tiny words stood out: Bat Night. Alvin felt the whole world was out to get him. Sisters, Lambies, cars, thermostats, mechanics, everything and everybody—they'd all ganged up just to make him miserable.

"The room's nice and clean," Mom said when she returned, "but it does seem awfully warm."

"That's 'cause you have to turn the air conditioner on to cool it off," said the manager.

Mr. Hoople asked what the room would cost, and the manager told him. "Sounds reasonable enough," said Dad, and while he filled out the registration card, Alvin and Annie and Mom helped Slim unload their bags in front of Room Number Three.

"I have to take Lambie to the bathroom," Annie said. Mom showed her the way.

Alvin lugged his suitcase through the door. The room felt like a giant pizza oven. "Where's that air conditioner?" he asked.

"Right under the window, it looks like." Dad pointed, hefting a suitcase. "See if you can figure out how it works."

Alvin didn't see any controls on the air conditioner. In fact, he wasn't sure it really *was* an air conditioner. But then he noticed a little fingerhole on top, and when he pulled up on it, a door popped open to reveal a secret panel full of push buttons.

Alvin pressed the button marked "COOL." The machine creaked into action and blew a stream of warm air at his face. He tried the button marked "SUPER COOL." That made the breeze even warmer.

"Is it working?" Dad asked.

"No. It's putting out hot air," Alvin complained.

"Maybe it just needs to warm up," Dad said, taking a look to make sure Alvin hadn't done something wrong.

"If it gets any warmer, we'll be roasted alive," Alvin griped. The heat was making him sick to his stomach.

Dad didn't have any luck with the air conditioner, either. Suddenly Alvin had an idea. He pushed the button marked "WARM." A blast of cold air rushed from the vents.

"I can feel it now," said Mom from across the room. "What'd you do?"

"You wouldn't believe me if I told you," Alvin said.

"Now that you've solved that problem, how would you like to hang up your clothes?" Mom asked.

"Not much," said Alvin, drying his underarms in the chilly breeze. "Besides what's the use of hanging them up if we're only going to pack them again in the morning anyhow?"

"Well, if you want people to call you 'Mr. Wrinkle,' it's fine with me," said Mom.

"Why not?" Alvin grumbled. "They certainly won't call me 'Mr. Baseball.' "

When he finished hanging up his clothes, Alvin took a tour of the motel room. Actually, there wasn't all that much to look at: two chairs that everybody in the United States and Canada seemed to have sat on, a desk with a lamp that rattled when anybody walked by, a faded color picture of the Grand Canyon, two cots, a big bed, a clothes closet without a door, and a TV set with a coin box.

"Twenty-five cents per hour!" Alvin exclaimed

when he read the instructions on the TV. "What a gyp!"

"Maybe we'll have a little peace and quiet tonight," Dad smiled. He hardly ever watched TV.

"But my favorite program's on at eight-thirty!" Alvin protested. "If I can't see the game, at least I should be able to watch TV."

"Well, you have your money. Is your program worth a quarter?"

When Dad put it that way, Alvin wasn't so sure. He thought he'd better give the matter careful consideration. After all, he didn't have to make his mind up till eight-twenty-nine, and maybe by then Mom and Dad would feel sorry for him and try to make up for Bat Night by treating him to some TV.

Alvin bounced up and down on the big bed till Mom asked him to stop. Then he noticed another coin box on the headboard. " 'Healthful Vibra-bed massages away your worries,' " he read. "Sounds like fun."

"What does that cost?" Mom asked.

Alvin took a closer look, "Twenty-five cents! Boy! Isn't anything free around here?"

"Of course," said Dad. "Here's your very own private drinking glass."

Alvin read its cellophane wrapper: " 'Your personal sanitary cup. With the compliments of the management.' "

"Sanitary!" Alvin snorted. "There's a big fingerprint on it!"

"Well, nobody's perfect," said Mom, handing him a plastic bucket. "Maybe you'd like to go get us some sanitary ice."

"How much do they charge for that?" Alvin wanted to know.

"Absolutely nothing," Dad said.

"I don't believe it!" Alvin retorted.

The machine was right outside the office and had a sign that said "FOR GUESTS ONLY" to keep other people from stealing the ice. Alvin was amazed it didn't have a coin slot. He opened the door, picked up the cold metal scoop inside, and tried to dig into a big pile of cubes. The ice was all stuck together and wouldn't budge. Alvin put down the bucket and used both hands on the scoop. He managed to chip one tiny cube loose, but the rest were frozen into a solid mass. He thought he'd better let the manager know.

He went into the office and walked up to the desk. "Your ice machine's broken," he said.

"What did you do to it?" grumped the manager.

"I didn't do anything to it," Alvin replied.

"Then how come it's broken?"

"I don't know. The ice is all stuck together."

"That doesn't mean the machine's broken. That's just how it works when it gets warm out."

"How do I get ice from it, then?"

"Use a little muscle," the manager recommended. "I'd help you, but it's too hot out there for a sane human being."

"Thanks," said Alvin sarcastically. He carried the empty ice bucket back to the room, where Annie was telling Lambie a story from one of her picture books. "Gimme some ice," she demanded.

"Here," said Alvin, handing her the bucket.

"Where is it?" she asked.

"It's invisible ice," he told her. "Bet you've never seen *that* before."

"Alvin, are you teasing me again?"

"Come on, Alvin. Where's the ice?" Mom asked.

"In the ice machine. It won't come out."

"Did you ask anybody for help?"

"Yeah, the manager, but he didn't want to bother."

Dad emerged from the bathroom. "What's the problem?"

"The ice is all stuck in the machine," Alvin told him.

"Well, I'll go see if I can chip some out," Dad said. "Why don't you wash up?"

This motel was beginning to get on Alvin's nerves. When he went into the bathroom and turned on the cold-water tap, he half expected scalding-hot water to come out. But the faucet delivered what it promised, and he washed his hands and face with the tiny motel soap. "Which towel's mine?" he shouted through the door. All the ones beside the basin looked exactly alike.

"The one on the bottom rack on the left," Mom shouted back.

"Somebody's already used that one," Alvin hollered.

"How about the one on the right?"

"I guess that one's okay." Alvin used it and went back into the room.

"Look what I found," Annie said proudly, holding up a fistful of postcards she'd discovered in the desk drawer.

Alvin took one. It had a picture of the motel on the

front. He flipped it over. " 'The Fine and Dandy Motel, Appleton, Pa.,' " he read. " 'Television. Vibra-beds. Free ice. Swimming.' "

"What's this about swimming?" Dad asked as he came through the door with the empty ice bucket.

"It says on this postcard that they have a swimming pool," Alvin explained.

"Let's see," Dad said. Annie handed him a postcard.

"If this place has a swimming pool, I'll eat my bathing suit," said Mom.

"But it says 'swimming,' " Alvin protested.

"It doesn't say swimming *pool,* though," Dad noticed.

"Maybe they mean you can swim in your bathtub," Mom remarked.

"I'll just pick up the phone and find out." Dad dialed the manager and asked if the motel had a swimming pool. He made funny faces while he listened to the answer. Then he said, "Thank you," and hung up.

"Well," Mom asked.

"Swimming costs only seventy-five cents per person at the municipal pool four or five blocks up the road. But he's pretty sure it's closed today for monthly cleaning."

"You know what?" Alvin pouted. "This place stinks."

8

While Dad was phoning Marty's parents to let them know about the change in plans, Alvin discovered a radio in the headboard behind his parents' bed. It was glued down so no one could steal it, but it didn't have a coin slot anywhere, so as far as Alvin could tell, it was absolutely free. "And that," he decided after he'd turned it on and waited for it to warm up and checked to make sure the plug was in the socket, "is probably why it doesn't work. Boy! I can't even *listen* to the ball game!"

Annie was very tired of playing with her bagful of Lambie and wondered what would happen if she opened his plastic prison and took just a tiny peek inside. "Don't do it," Mom warned when she noticed Annie fiddling with the tape that sealed Lambie in. Annie took her advice, even though she desperately wished she could give Lambie a sniff and find out what he smelled like. The bag didn't smell like much of anything at all.

Dad hung up the phone. "They're very disappointed we won't be there tonight."

"*They're* disappointed!" Alvin snorted.

"Betsy said she had a big supper planned for us."

"Don't worry, Dad. Marty'll be able to finish it off for her."

"That's not a nice thing to say," Mom scolded as she took off her shoes and lay down on the bed.

"But he's a tub," Alvin pointed out.

"You shouldn't make fun of people," Mom insisted.

"No, you shouldn't," Annie agreed, "even if they are tubs. You know what? I'm bored."

So was Alvin, now that he'd explored the entire room and its contents. "Let's take a walk," he suggested, itching to see whether the rest of Appleton had more to offer than the Fine and Dandy Motel. If he couldn't go to the ball game, at least he could do something more exciting than sit around in a dumb motel room.

"Wouldn't you like to lie down for a while?" Mom asked. "It's hot enough to fry bacon on the pavement out there"

"I want to go for a walk," said Annie. Mom groaned and put her shoes back on.

"Are you sure you want to do this?" she asked when she stepped out the door and felt the withering heat. Before anybody could answer her, a fluffy gray-and-white kitten bounded up to Annie and snuggled against her ankles.

Annie was delighted. "Hello, kitty," she said, dropping her Lambie bag to pet the friendly newcomer. He started to purr. "You're a very nice little kitten," said Annie.

Mom petted him, too. "I wonder who he belongs to."

"The manager?" Alvin suggested.

"Somehow, I don't think he's the kitten type," Dad said.

"Maybe he belongs to one of the other guests," Mom thought.

"We're the only guests in this joint," Alvin pointed out.

"Could be a stray," Dad said, "but he seems well fed."

"Nice kitty," said Annie, stroking the fur behind his neck.

Alvin was getting impatient. This was a vacation, after all. You could pet kittens anyplace, but you couldn't tour downtown Appleton every day. "What about our walk?" he asked.

"Come on, Annie," said Mom, starting down the path with Dad and Alvin. Annie gave the kitten a few parting caresses and caught up.

"Didn't you forget something?" Mom asked.

"Huh?" said Annie. "Oh!" And she ran back to rescue Lambie from the hot pavement.

With his excellent sense of direction, Alvin remembered exactly how to get back into town, so he led the way. After passing some little businesses they came to the municipal park, where, sure enough, two men with long-handled brushes were giving the empty swimming pool a good scrubdown.

A few yards beyond, Annie spotted a sliding board, and before anybody could stop her, she was on her way to the top. Mom and Dad decided that this playground would be an excellent place to rest their weary bones, so they sat on the swings while Annie slid on the slide and Alvin climbed the monkey bars.

As he was coming down from the top, Alvin nearly stepped on the fingers of a red-haired kid clambering up. "Watch it!" shouted the red-haired kid, who, though a lot shorter, looked about Alvin's age.

"Sorry," Alvin apologized.

"Hey, I never saw you before. Did you just move in?" asked the red-haired kid.

"We're just staying here for the night," Alvin explained. "We were on our way to Philadelphia, but our car broke down."

"Where do you live?"

"Sherwood Forest, New York."

"Never heard of it," said the redhead, pulling himself between two rungs and swinging by one arm.

"Well, I never heard of Appleton till we got stuck here," Alvin pointed out.

"But Appleton is the home of the Appleton Apple Festival," said the red-haired kid. "You've heard of that."

"No, I haven't," said Alvin, climbing up to the top again.

"Boy are you ignorant! Everybody's heard of the Appleton Apple Festival."

"Maybe everybody in Appleton's heard of it, but it sure isn't a big deal anywhere else."

"That's what *you* think," said the red-haired kid, walking with his hands from rung to rung. "It's even on television."

"So is the Sherwood Forest Sewer Service, but I wouldn't call that a big deal, either," Alvin replied.

From the top of the monkey bars, Alvin could see clear across the park. At the other end, a bunch of kids in uniforms were taking fielding practice. "Is that your baseball league?" Alvin asked.

"Yeah," said the red-haired kid. "Do you have one where you come from?"

"My team's in second place," Alvin said proudly.

"My team's lost every game we've played," laughed the redhead. "We're putrid."

"Do you collect baseball cards?" Alvin asked.

"Sure."

"Do you have Wayne McGonigle? Number 337?"

"I've got 'em all."

Alvin couldn't believe his ears. Wayne McGonigle was the only player he needed to complete his collection. Maybe this trip wouldn't turn out so badly after all. "You want to trade for him?"

"Maybe. What'll you give me?"

"Who do you want?"

"How about some team cards: the Orioles, the Pirates, the Phillies, and the Mets. Plus maybe the Yankees."

"That's an awful lot for McGonigle. He's not that great a player."

"Take it or leave it."

"Where are your cards?" Alvin asked.

"Up at my house. Where are yours?"

"At the motel. Can you come by after dinner?"

"Let's go, Alvin!" shouted Mr. Hoople, waving to his son.

"Just a second!" Alvin yelled back. "You want to come over later?" he asked the red-haired kid.

"I've got a game tonight at seven-thirty. Maybe I

could come over before that. Which motel are you staying at?''

"It's room three," Alvin said, but for some reason he couldn't remember the name of the place. "The Stinky Motel" was what kept running through his mind, but he knew that wasn't right. Then it came to him: "The Fine and Dandy."

"That dump?"

"Alvin!" Dad shouted.

"Just a second!" Alvin hollered back, and turned to the red-haired kid. "Come around seven and be sure to bring your McGonigle."

"I'll try," said the red-haired kid. "I guess your name's Alvin, huh?"

"Yeah. What's yours?"

"Fred Eichelberger. See you later, maybe."

"Alvin!" Dad thundered. Alvin scrambled down the monkey bars and headed toward the swings.

"What took you so long?" his mother asked.

"That kid over there has some cards I need. He's gonna come by the motel at seven or so, and we're gonna trade."

"What if we're somewhere else at seven?" Dad asked.

"But we have to be back," Alvin insisted. "I told him I'd be there."

"Well, we'll see," Dad said.

Alvin got worried. When Dad said "We'll see," it usually meant "Don't count on it." And losing a Phillies bat and a Wayne McGonigle card in one evening, Alvin thought, would be a greater disaster than he could possibly stand. His stomach started feeling funny again.

9

But it made a miraculous recovery. Appleton's dinnertime had arrived, and as he and his family walked down a shady residential street, Alvin could smell charcoal on somebody's barbecue. A sudden whiff of hot dogs reminded him he hadn't eaten anything since that sundae. "I'm hungry," he announced as they reached the center of town.

"Me, too," said Annie.

"Well, let's take a little stroll before dinner," Dad said. "Maybe we'll find a nice restaurant."

They turned up Delicious Street, downtown Appleton's main thoroughfare. The sign on the bank said it was 00 degrees. Alvin guessed it really meant 100 degrees but the 1 wasn't working. Either that, or the sign showed the temperature at the North Pole.

Across the street, the theater was showing a super horror double bill: *The Bog Monster* and *Dinosaur Attack*. "Could we go see those tonight?" Alvin asked.

"Don't you have to be back at the motel to meet your friend?" Dad reminded him.

"Oh, yeah." Alvin shrugged, suddenly wondering whether five cards for a second-string player like McGonigle was such a good deal after all. "Maybe we could go see the late show."

"Frankly, Alvin," Mom said, "I doubt these pictures will be masterpieces."

"They might be fun, though," Alvin protested, but he got the feeling he had about as much chance of seeing bog monsters or attacking dinosaurs tonight as he had of seeing the Phillies.

Annie was mumbling to herself the way she often did, when suddenly she stopped in front of an auto supply store and pointed to a tricycle in the window. "Let's get one of those!" she suggested.

"Where would we put it?" Dad asked.

"We could tie it to our car just like they tied our car to that truck."

Nobody else seemed to think much of that idea, so Annie started mumbling again, and Mom took her into the five-and-ten, where they looked for some emery boards Mom needed. In the meantime, Dad and Alvin stepped inside the sporting-goods shop next door.

Alvin was impressed. He'd never seen such a collection of baseball gloves. And bats! They seemed to have an autographed bat for every player in the major leagues except Wayne McGonigle. "May I help you?" asked a potbellied man in a wrinkly leisure suit.

"I guess we're just looking. Or are we, Dad?" Alvin asked, hoping Mr. Hoople might take the hint and buy him something.

"Yes, indeedy," Dad replied, swinging a shiny

metal tennis racket as if he wouldn't mind owning it. "Where's the best place to get dinner around here?"

"Depends on what you're looking for," the man replied. "For big full-course meals, you could try Winkle's over on McIntosh Street. That's two blocks back of the theater. Or if you're looking for seafood, there's Mr. Clam, down on Cortland Avenue at the corner of Winesap. Whatever you do, don't miss out on the deep-dish apple pie. It's our local specialty. What do you think of that racket?"

"Terrific," Dad said. "How much is it?"

"Special this week only. Sixty-nine ninety-five. Regularly eighty-nine fifty."

"Oh," said Dad, setting it down. "Guess I don't like it as much as I thought."

"This bat's only three ninety-five, Dad," said Alvin, nearly knocking over a display of fishing rods with his practice swing. "And it's autographed by Willie Flashner." Willie Flashner was Alvin's favorite Phillie.

"I don't know," Dad said.

"It's not the same as a Bat Night bat," Alvin said, "but it's pretty nice."

"You win," Dad said, and paid the salesman for the bat. "Thanks," Alvin said, taking a cut that just missed the cash register. "This is a really neat bat."

"You're quite welcome," Dad replied, "but I'd appreciate it if you'd save your batting practice for the ball park."

"Shall I wrap it up?" the salesman asked.

"No, thanks," Alvin said. "I'll just carry it like this."

"Well, be careful," the salesman advised. "With

that Phillies cap and that new bat, you never know when somebody might come up and ask you for your autograph.''

Alvin grinned. He knew the salesman was probably kidding. Still, when he went outside and looked at his reflection in the store's plate-glass window, he decided he did resemble Willie Flashner quite a bit. But Annie didn't ask him for his autograph. She had somehow wheedled Mom into buying her a coloring book, and she insisted on showing Alvin every single picture even though he wasn't the least bit interested.

Alvin thought a big full-course meal at Winkle's would really hit the spot, but Dad and Mom were in the mood for seafood, so Alvin led the way to Mr. Clam. Mom wanted to stop and ask directions, but Alvin pointed down the block. There in the distance, a happy clam smiled down at them.

Like gentlemen, Dad and Alvin held the door for Mom and Annie, and Dad made Alvin take off his Phillies cap before he went in. The sun outside was so bright and the restaurant so dark that Alvin could hardly see when he first stepped through the door. But when his eyes adjusted, he discovered that the whole place was decorated with fishnets and anchors and ships' steering wheels and big stuffed fish and even what appeared to be a real sailboat. It looked like fun.

While they were waiting for the hostess, Annie looked up toward the cash register and noticed a toothpick dispenser exactly like the one she remembered from this morning. Luckily for everybody, Alvin saw her reach toward it and grabbed her arm away before she could do any damage. Annie gave him her very meanest scowl, but Dad quietly patted him on the back and said, "Thanks, pal."

The hostess showed them to a pleasant booth under a shark and gave them each a menu shaped like a fish. "I don't like fish," Annie declared. This was news to the rest of the family, since she had eaten quite a few in her time.

"If that's how you feel about it," Dad replied, "you may have a one-hundred-percent all-beef hamburger."

"Good," said Annie. "I don't like fish."

Alvin couldn't decide between fish and seafood, so Dad suggested he order the flounder stuffed with crabmeat, and when the waitress came over, that's exactly what he did. Dad ordered trout, and Mom decided on the soft-shell crab. Then Dad asked for a hamburger and French fries for Annie. "I don't want a hamburg," she announced. "I want fish."

"I thought you didn't like fish," Mom reminded her.

"I do now," said Annie.

Dad told the waitress his daughter would have the halibut. "No, no!" cried Annie. "I want fish."

"Halibut *is* fish," Alvin told her.

"Oh," said Annie. The waitress asked her if she'd prefer a baked potato or French fries.

Annie gave the matter much thought. "A baked potato, please," she said finally.

"All righty," said the waitress. She was about to step into the kitchen when she heard Annie shout "No! French fries!" The waitress nodded, scratched out the baked potato, and scurried into the kitchen before Annie could change her mind again.

"Help yourself to all you can eat from our Sailboat Salad Bar with every dinner," read the spine of the menufish. Dad got up and led the way. Alvin's eyes hadn't deceived him: At the other end of the dining room was a real sailboat with bowls and bowls of different kinds of food all along the deck. The only time Alvin had ever seen anything like it was when the Hooples went to a smorgasbord. But the smorgasbord wasn't in a sailboat.

What you were supposed to do, Dad explained, was take a clean bowl from the pile and make your own salad with whatever you wanted. Alvin took some lettuce to start with, then added cherry tomatoes, beets, cauliflower, and some cubes of toasted bread. He didn't take any cucumbers, because he didn't like cucumbers. "What are those?" he asked, pointing to a bowlful of some little round brown things he didn't recognize.

"Chickpeas," Dad said.

"Do they taste like chicken?"

"Try some and see."

Alvin put some in his bowl. He figured they couldn't be any worse than cucumbers.

"Are you supposed to put *that* on your salad?" Alvin asked, pointing to an enormous bowl of applesauce.

"That's what the little plates are for," Mom informed him. Alvin set his salad bowl down on the edge of the boat. He took a plate and helped himself to applesauce and coleslaw and some yellow-and-red stuff that Dad said was corn relish. Then he noticed a long loaf of homemade bread at the sailboat's stern. He took his plate over, picked up the knife, carefully sliced himself a good-sized hunk of bread, and put five or six curls of butter on his plate to go with it. Then he went back to his bowl and ladled gobs and gobs of dressing onto his salad.

Balancing the bowl in one hand and the plate in the other, he slowly made his way back to the booth. Mom closed her eyes: She could just picture Alvin tripping over his shoelaces and dropping applesauce down somebody's neck. But Alvin got to the booth without spilling a drop. He thought when he grew up and became a major leaguer he might work as a waiter in the wintertime.

Annie was having trouble trying to decide exactly what she liked and what she didn't, but Mom and Dad finally got her squared away and returned to the booth. Alvin was already busy wolfing down his salad.

"What kind of dressing is that?" Mom asked.

"French, thousand island, Italian, and blue cheese, all mixed together."

"Alvin, how could you?"

"Try some," he offered.

"No, thank you, sir," said Mom.

Alvin thought the combination was delicious. After all, he'd invented it himself. The corn relish and the chickpeas weren't bad, either. In fact, everything was so good, Alvin went back for seconds. Dad did, too, except for the applesauce; after all, he had his weight to consider.

Alvin was ready to go back for thirds, but Dad suggested he save room for the rest of his dinner. Fortunately for poor starving Alvin, it arrived a moment later.

"Yuck!" Annie winced when she saw Mom's plate. "What's that ugly thing?"

"That is a crab," Mom said. "Would you like to taste some?"

"No," said Annie. "It looks yucky."

"In general," Dad pointed out, "when you think someone else's food looks yucky, it's a good idea to keep it to yourself so you don't spoil her dinner."

"I'm sorry," said Annie. Taking another look at Mom's crab, she just kept quiet and made a very ugly face.

The waitress set Annie's halibut filet in front of her. "This isn't fish!" Annie complained.

"Of course it is," said Mom. "And I'll bet it's delicious."

"But where's its eyes? Where's its tail? I want a fish like Dad's."

"Annie," Dad said as patiently as he could, "my fish is a whole trout with a lot of bones in it. What you have is part of a big fish like that one up there on the wall. The chef has gone to the trouble of removing the skin and bones for you, which when you think about it is really rather nice of him. Now, enjoy your dinner."

"But I want a whole fish."

"Do you really think you could eat a whole fish that size?"

"I could try."

"Why don't you try to eat the fish you've got?"

"Okay."

"Could I have a little taste of that crab?" Dad asked Mom.

Mom frowned. "Must you?"

76

"Don't be shellfish, Mom," Alvin teased. His parents groaned.

Alvin's stuffed flounder was every bit as tasty as his salad creation. And the homemade deep-dish apple pie was so delicious he could've found room for another two or three pieces if he hadn't gone overboard earlier at the Sailboat Salad Bar.

When it was time to leave, he was so full he could barely stand up. "That was some meal," he burped, grabbing his bat.

"Glad you enjoyed it," said Dad.

"I liked mine, too," said Annie, "even if it didn't have any eyes."

Dad paid the check. The hostess offered everybody some little white after-dinner mints. Mom made sure Annie steered clear of the toothpick dispenser. The well-stuffed family was all ready to leave when Annie uttered the familiar words, "Where's Lambie?"

"You didn't bring him," said Alvin.

"Yes, I did," said Annie. "He went on the slide with me."

"Uh-oh," Dad muttered, guessing what that must mean.

"I don't think you had him in the five-and-ten," Mom said.

"I don't remember," Annie replied, puzzled.

"You must've left him at the playground," Mom said. "We'll go back and look."

For a minute, Annie acted almost grown up. She didn't scream "I want my Lambie!" until everybody got out the door. But after that, she kept shrieking it over and over again until Dad finally cheered her up a little by carrying her piggyback. There are a lot of bad things about being little, Alvin thought with a slight twinge of jealousy, but getting piggyback rides isn't one of them.

When they got back to the playground, another ball game was in the third inning, and the men at the swimming pool were watching it fill up with water. Annie ran over to the slide and looked for Lambie, but she couldn't find him anywhere. Mom and Dad asked the kids playing there if they'd seen a plastic bag with what looked like a greasy oil rag inside, but none of them had.

"Maybe somebody threw him away," Alvin suggested, and he and his parents began rummaging through the trash barrels. "This sure must look funny," Alvin observed.

"It's not a bit funny," Annie screamed. To her it was terrible.

Mom and Dad and Alvin found everything from broken shoelaces to used hunks of bubble gum in the rubbish, but the one thing they didn't find was Lambie. Annie started to weep again.

"We'll get you another Lambie," Dad said, trying to comfort her. "A clean one with fluffy fur."

"But he won't be the same," Annie bawled.

"Who knows? He might even be nicer."

"I doubt it," Annie sobbed.

Dad picked her up and hoisted her to his shoulders. She sniffled all the way back to the motel. Lambie was gone forever. Just like Bat Night, Alvin thought sadly.

10

"Hey, that kitten's still here!" cried Alvin. The little stray was pawing at the door of their motel room.

"Maybe he wants to get in out of the heat," said Dad, carefully digging the room key out of his pocket while trying to keep Annie balanced on his shoulders.

The instant Dad opened the door, Alvin rushed inside so he could beat everyone else to the bathroom. The kitten scampered in, too, and hid under Annie's cot.

Mom smiled. "Maybe we should get an extra bed."

Dad hoisted Annie down from his shoulders. She lay across the cot on her stomach and leaned over to look at the kitten. "Hello, kitty," said Annie. The kitten backed away. "I'm your friend," she said. "Please come here."

The little stray crept toward her hesitantly. He was almost in her hands when a loud knock at the door scared him back under the cot again.

Mom went to see who it was. Standing at the door was a short red-haired kid in a well-worn baseball uniform that said "Macs" in big red letters across the front. "I'm Fred Eichelberger," he said. "Is Alvin here?"

"He sure is," said Mrs. Hoople. "A Mr. Eichelberger to see you, Alvin!" she yelled.

Alvin came out of the bathroom. "Got your cards?" Fred asked him.

"Sure," said Alvin, trying to remember where he'd left them. "Hang on a second."

He reached under the desk and brought out his shoebox. "Let's go outside," he said, preferring not to have his parents listen in on his private transactions. "I'll be right out there if you need me," he told Mom.

"Have fun," she said.

"Want to flip some?" Fred asked when they got outside.

"Maybe later. Let's see your McGonigle."

"Right here," said Fred, snapping a red rubber band from a tall stack of cards. He showed Alvin the McGonigle. It was the card Alvin wanted, all right, but it looked as though it'd gone through the laundry in somebody's blue jeans and gotten stepped on by somebody's baseball shoes. Which, in fact, it had. Sometimes Fred forgot to empty his pockets before his pants got washed, and once in a while he carelessly left some of his cards on the bedroom floor.

"This card's in crummy shape," Alvin told him. "Don't you have a double of him?"

"This *is* my double. Do you want him or not?"

"He's not worth any five cards in that condition."

"What'll you give me?"

80

"I guess I could give you one of those teams you wanted."

"One!" cried Fred, acting astonished. "Four's more like it!"

"That McGonigle's a mess. Two, maybe, but that's all."

Fred thought it over. "Okay. The Yankees and the Phillies."

Alvin thumbed through his collection. "Okay on the Yankees. I don't have doubles of the Phillies."

"But they're the ones I really wanted. It'll take two to replace 'em."

"Which two?"

"The Orioles and the Reds."

This deal wasn't turning out the way Alvin had hoped. "I don't know . . ."

"Do you want McGonigle or don't you?"

Alvin discovered he had quadruples of the Orioles and quintuples of the Reds. "Okay. It's a deal," he said. "Those three for McGonigle." He held out his cards in one hand and took Fred's mashed-up McGonigle with the other.

"What else do you need?" asked Fred.

"Nobody now," said Alvin. "McGonigle completes my set. I've been looking all over for this card."

"Boy, if I knew that, I'd've gotten a lot more than three for him," said Fred.

Alvin grinned. "I know. That's why I didn't mention it."

"How many cards do you have?" Fred asked.

"I never kept track. Eight or nine hundred, maybe."

"I have three thousand two hundred and thirty-four. Plus your three, minus McGonigle. Three thousand two hundred and thirty-six."

"That's a lot of cards," Alvin admitted.

"The most of anybody I know," Fred bragged. "Sure you don't want to flip some?"

Alvin figured anybody who had three thousand two hundred and however many odd cards was probably a terrific flipper. Maybe because he was so close to the ground. "No, thanks," said Alvin.

"You sure?"

"Positive."

"Want to come watch me play? We're playing the Winesaps in half an hour."

"Where do you get names like that?" Alvin wanted to know.

"Like what?"

"Winesaps. Macs. I've never heard of baseball teams with those names before."

"In Appleton, every team's named after a different kind of apple."

"Weird," Alvin mumbled.

"It's neat, unless you have to be on the Granny Smiths," Fred said. "Do you want to come to the game?"

"Does it cost anything?"

"Of course not."

"Let me see if it's okay. I'll be right back." Alvin stepped into the motel room.

"Foo!" cried Annie, still leaning over her cot. "You scared kitty again!"

"I didn't mean to," Alvin apologized. He turned toward his parents, who were lying on the bed reading the newspaper. "Can I go watch Fred's ball game?"

"Won't you miss your favorite program?" Dad asked.

"I can see that any old week. Besides, it'd cost a quarter. The game's free."

"Can't argue when the price is right," Dad said. "Enjoy yourself. I'll come join you later on."

"You don't have to if you don't want to," Alvin said thoughtfully. He knew his dad didn't care much for baseball.

"You wait there till Dad comes for you," Mom said. "It's light now, but I don't want you to walk home alone in the dark along that highway."

"Okay," said Alvin, picking up his mitt in case any foul balls should come his way. He thought about taking his bat, too, but he decided it'd be safer in the room.

Outside, Alvin found Fred sharpening his card-flipping skills. "I just won ten from myself," Fred chuckled, and kneeled down to pick them up.

As he and Alvin walked toward the park, Fred went into great detail about the famous Appleton Apple Festival. It was held every fall, and it had carnival rides and games and contests, plus everything you could think of that was made from apples: dumplings, fritters, pies, cobbler, cider, cake, cookies, pan dowdy, and stuff Fred couldn't remember. The way he described it made it sound as though it really ought to be famous.

In fact, it made Alvin hungry again, even though he'd eaten such a huge dinner just a little while ago. One of the older kids had just what he needed: ice balls. The tall kid made them in a little red wagon next to the grandstand, which didn't seem all that sanitary, but those ice balls sure looked tempting in this stifling heat.

"How much?" Alvin asked.

"Fifteen cents," said the Ice Ball King. It sounded a little high to Alvin, but he figured that since he wasn't spending that quarter on the TV, he'd still be a dime ahead.

"Okay," Alvin said.

The tall kid chipped a hunk of ice from a big block, put it in the crusher, and turned the handle. A stream of ice flowed into a paper cone, and the vendor shaped it into a neat round ball. "What flavor?" he asked.

The wagon was full of bottles of syrup of every color under the sun. Orange, blue, purple, green, red, yellow, chartreuse—Alvin couldn't decide. "It's melting," the kid told him. "Better make up your mind."

"Can I have a little of each?" Alvin asked.

"Sure. No extra charge." The iceman put a few drops of each syrup on Alvin's ice ball. Alvin handed him a quarter, and he made change from a little metal machine on his belt.

"Don't you want one?" Alvin asked Fred.

"Not me," Fred replied. "The last time I had one right before a game, I threw up in the second inning."

Alvin found a seat at the very top of the grandstand. The lights came on, and the Macs took the field. Fred waved to Alvin from second base, and Alvin waved back. The umpire hollered, "Batter up!" and the game got started.

The Winesaps took the lead right away on a couple of base hits, a home run, and six or seven errors, three of them by Fred. He let a hot grounder roll between his legs, he dropped an easy pop fly, and he kicked a slow roller as if it were a football. "He may be Appleton's champion card flipper," thought Alvin, "but he sure isn't their champion second baseman."

Fred wasn't any marvel with the bat, either. His first time up, he fouled one off right into Alvin's glove. The fans gave Alvin a hand for his excellent catch. Alvin wished he could keep the ball as a souvenir of his vacation, but he knew from his own league that he had to throw it back.

Fred struck out on a pitch that bounced in front of the plate, and the inning was over. Alvin heard a rumbling overhead that sounded like an airplane, but when he looked up and saw some lightning, he decided it must be thunder.

By the end of the second inning, the poor Macs were down eleven to nothing, and all they could do was stare up at the clouds and pray that it'd rain soon and wash out the game. It was seventeen to nothing in the top of the third when their prayers were answered. The air got heavier, the thunder boomed, the sky cracked open, and big warm raindrops pelted the field.

Alvin remembered what he'd learned about lightning striking the tallest objects, so he scrambled down from the grandstand and squatted near the foul line. He wondered what he should do next. The rain was coming down harder now, and there wasn't anyplace nearby to take cover. He remembered what Mom said about waiting for Dad, but she didn't say what to do if it rained and Dad was nowhere in sight. When a muddy one-hopper bounced off Fred's chest and the umpire yelled, "Game called on account of rain!" Alvin decided he'd better run for it.

He dashed his hardest as the thunder cracked all around him and the rain soaked through his shirt. By the time he reached a little grocery store halfway to the motel, he couldn't run another step. He stopped under the awning to catch his breath. As he puffed and panted, he saw a familiar figure hurry through the parking lot toward the baseball field. "Dad!" Alvin shouted between gasps. "I'm over here!"

Mr. Hoople stopped in his tracks and ran toward the awning. "Quite a cloudburst," he panted.

"I'll say," said Alvin. "I waited for you."

"I was in the shower," Dad wheezed.

"Looks like you're in one again."

"You said it, buster." Dad was every bit as wet as Alvin, and he dripped as he talked. "This place seems to be open. As long as we're stuck here, do you want anything to eat?"

Alvin decided not to say anything about the ice ball he'd had at the game. "I wouldn't mind a fudge bar or something."

"Well, let's see if we can rustle up a couple."

Dad was treating, so Alvin didn't think it'd be polite to mention his diet. By the time they finished their fudge bars, the rain had changed to hailstones. "Well, at least we won't get any wetter, though we may get conked in the noggin," Dad said. "Let's

86

go!'' He ran down the road toward the motel with Alvin right behind him.

"Shhhh!" Mom whispered, putting her fingers to her lips as Dad and Alvin came through the door. "Annie's trying to fall asleep."

"No, I'm not," Annie said truthfully. She was actually watching the kitten bat the curtain pulls back and forth.

"You'd better be," Mom scolded.

"Hey, you're all wet!" Annie exclaimed when she saw Dad and Alvin.

"You get to sleep," Dad told her, dripping a little as he kissed her on the forehead. He grabbed a towel from the bathroom and started drying his hair.

"Your pajamas are on the bed," Mom told Alvin. "Get out of those wet things and take a shower."

"But I just got one," Alvin said.

"Now try one with soap," Mom ordered.

Alvin wasn't used to the motel shower, and it took him quite a while to get it adjusted. First it was too cold. Then it was too hot and too hard. He got it just right, but when he stepped in, it turned cold again.

At last he got it just the way he liked it. As he lathered and rinsed, he sang some of the songs he'd heard on the radio today. Dad stuck his head in the door and asked him to sing a little softer, since Annie was almost asleep.

"No, I'm not," Alvin heard Annie shout.

"Better hurry!" Dad chided her.

Alvin finished his shower, found what he hoped was his towel, and dried himself off. Then he got into his pajamas, brushed and flossed his teeth, and went back into the room. Dad was playing with the kitten on the floor. He'd dangle a piece of dental floss, and the kitten would pounce on it.

"Is he going to sleep with us?" Alvin asked.

"If he doesn't make too much of a racket," Dad said softly. "It's too wet to put him out, and besides, he seems to like us."

"Who does he belong to?"

"The manager doesn't have any idea. We looked in the local paper, but there weren't any ads for lost kittens. Somebody may have deserted this one to get rid of him. People do that sometimes."

"Are we going to keep him?" Alvin asked, noticing a soap dish full of milk on the floor.

"Oh, we'll see," said Dad.

There's nothing harder to do than fall asleep in a lumpy cot when your sister's snoring in the one beside you. Alvin tried and tried, but it wasn't until Annie finally rolled over and stopped sawing wood that he finally dozed off. Just then the kitten pounced on his ear, and he had to fall asleep all over again.

Brrzap! In the middle of the night, when everbody was sound asleep. the Vibra-bed suddenly buzzed into action. The kitten yowled, and Alvin and Annie woke up to see Mom and Dad bouncing uncontrollably back and forth as the mad bed bucked and jostled them.

Alvin howled with laughter. "At least we got one bargain in this place!" he shouted. Dad finally pulled the plug, but by then Alvin and Annie were laughing so hard it took them a long time to simmer down and go back to sleep. And when they did, they dreamed of Vibra-beds all night long.

11

What woke Alvin in the morning was Annie's yelling. She was going "Here, kitty, kitty!" all around the room, and when she didn't find him, she shouted. "Where are you, kitty?" at the top of her lungs.

That woke Mom and Dad. They explained they'd put the cat outside in the middle of the night when he decided to use their backs to sharpen his claws.

Annie opened the door. Before she could say, "Here, kitty!" the spunky animal bounced into the room and snuggled up against her legs.

"Let's take him home with us!" she cried.

"Let's think about it," said Mom.

While everybody was getting dressed and washed and packed, the kitten jumped inside one of the suitcases. Dad put him back on the floor before he could scratch any of the clothes, and then he made sure all the bags were locked tight. They left the kitten in the room and strolled to Winkle's for a full-course breakfast.

Alvin's waffles were at least as good as yesterday's hotcakes, even though they came with only two kinds of syrup. Dad abandoned his diet entirely and ordered an enormous breakfast with "pigs in blankets," which Annie was very disappointed to discover were really only sausages wrapped up in pancakes. She'd expected to see warm pink animals crying "Oink!" in their little beds.

After breakfast, Mom and Annie ambled back to the motel while Dad and Alvin hiked to Slim's Super Service Station. "What happened to our car?" Alvin wondered. From a distance, it looked as though the trunk was all bashed in.

"Oh, no!" Dad groaned, walking faster and expecting the worst. "I hope that's not an example of their Super Service!"

Then Alvin noticed something important. "That car's got a Pennsylvania license plate!" he observed. "It looks like ours, but it must be someone else's."

Dad breathed a sigh of relief. Alvin was right again. Their car was on the other side of the pumps, and it looked fine. Marlin was pouring coolant into their radiator. "Just about finished," he said. "You should be all set."

Alvin stepped inside the office and browsed through the road-map display. He found a map of Delaware and brought it outside with him. "How much is this?" he asked Marlin.

"Seventy-five cents, usually, but seeing as how you're such good customers, it'll be on the house." Marlin winked.

"Does that mean free?" Alvin asked.

"One hundred and fifty percent."

"Thank you," Alvin said. "I collect maps, and I don't have one of Delaware. You wouldn't have one of Colorado, would you?"

"I'm afraid not," said Marlin. "Ohio's as far west as we get."

"That's a shame," Alvin said. "I already have a map of Ohio."

Dad settled the bill, and they got into the car. "Hope it doesn't give us any more trouble," Dad said, turning the ignition key. The engine started right up. Dad broke into a big smile. He and Alvin drove back to the motel.

"Well, we're all set," Dad said as he entered the room.

"We are, too," Mom said. "Everything's packed."

"What about our kitty?" Annie asked.

Dad smiled. "Somehow, I thought you'd bring that up."

"He'd make a very nice pet," Annie said. "I don't have any pets now that Lambie's dead."

"What about your goldfish?" Mom asked.

"Cats are cuddlier," said Annie.

"Why don't we get a Saint Bernard?" Alvin asked. He always thought that if you were going to have a pet, it was a good idea to have one that could rescue you in a snowstorm.

"Don't you like this kitten?" Mom asked.

"He's okay, I guess," Alvin said. "But he's no Saint Bernard."

"As far as I'm concerned, that's a point in his favor," said Dad. "Maybe we should take him with us."

"Oh, boy!" Annie squealed. "I love you, kitty!" And she picked him up and squeezed him so tightly that Dad had to remind her that there's a difference between real animals and stuffed toys.

91

"I knew that," Annie said, "but I forgot."

They left the kitten in the motel room and drove downtown to the pet store to buy him a cage. But when they got there, the sign on the door said "CLOSED." Everybody stood on the sidewalk while Mom and Dad tried to decide what to do, and just as they were about to look elsewhere, a thin man with a thin black mustache let them in.

"How can I help you, folks?" he asked. Mom explained about the new kitten, and before she knew it, she'd bought a wood-and-wire carrier, a box of kitten food, a bag of kitty litter, two dishes, a leash, and a book on cat care. Annie thought they should get a fancy carpeted tree house that went from the floor to the ceiling, but Dad pointed out how difficult it would be to fit it into the trunk. As it was, most of the kitty gear had to go into the backseat.

When they returned to the motel, the Hooples found their new pet hanging by his claws from the top of the curtains. "Never a dull moment," Mom sighed. She unstuck him and set him down on the floor, and he ran right up the curtains again.

Alvin went to the bathroom and discovered the kitten had used the tub for a toilet. "I'm beginning to see why the motel manager doesn't care for animals," said Dad as he cleaned up the mess.

Meanwhile, Annie and Alvin showed the kitten his new cage. The minute he saw it, he scampered under the double bed and hid where nobody could reach him.

"Please come out," Annie begged.

"Here, kitty," Alvin coaxed from the other side.

"Come on, feline. Time to go," said Mom, crouching at the end of the bed.

But Dad knew a few things about kittens. He stooped down, put some kitten food in his hand, and held it under the bed. That did the trick. When the kitten rushed up for his breakfast, Dad snatched him up and locked him in the carrier. Then everybody got up off the floor, Dad went to pay the bill, Alvin helped Mom arrange the suitcases in the trunk, and they were off for Philadelphia once more.

It was supposed to be a two-hour drive to Marty's house, but it actually took a little longer. The kitten didn't like the car at first, and when Annie took him out of the carrier to comfort him, he got loose and ran up Dad's pant leg. They had to stop till they could get him back into the cage, and Mom and Dad made Annie promise not to touch him again until they got to Philadelphia.

Everybody agreed the kitten deserved a name.

"Let's call him 'Appleton Mac,' " Alvin suggested.

"How about 'Fred Eichelberger?' " Mom asked.

"I know!" cried Annie. "Let's call him 'Lambie'!"

"That," said Alvin, "is the dumbest thing I have ever heard."

Mom and Dad and Annie outvoted him anyway. Alvin was furious, but Lambie the Second didn't seem to mind his new name at all.

By the time they saw the first signs pointing to Philadelphia, it was beginning to get hot again. Alvin unfolded his maps and helped navigate Dad to Ardmore, the suburb where Cousin Marty's family lived. Unfortunately, they navigated into a colossal traffic jam, and they inched forward irritably in the heat and humidity and exhaust for an hour and a half before they could get off the not-so-superhighway.

They passed seven or eight gas stations and a shopping center and got lost and had to turn around in a supermarket parking lot, but finally they found the right street, and a minute later they were parked in Cousin Marty's driveway.

Marty's mother hugged and kissed everybody and remarked on how big Annie and Alvin had grown, and then Mr. and Mrs. Hoople said the same thing about Marty, which Alvin thought was pretty funny, since Marty was tubbier than ever. At last the whole hungry crew went to the backyard for a picnic.

Marty's mother had fixed lemonade and potato salad and bologna sandwiches. Alvin didn't like bologna much, but he ate it to be polite. Annie didn't care for it, either, but she wasn't the least bit bashful about saying so. "I hate bologna!" said she, so Marty's mother made her a special cheese sandwich instead. It looked so much tastier than bologna that Alvin wished he'd said something himself.

"Did you hear who won the Phillies game last night?" Alvin asked Marty.

"I don't pay any attention to baseball," Marty replied with his mouth full.

"It poured all afternoon and evening yesterday," Marty's mother told Alvin. "They called off the game."

"You mean it was rained out?" Alvin asked. "They couldn't have Bat Night?"

"I guess they had to postpone it."

"Does that mean Bat Night's tonight?" Alvin asked.

"I suppose so," she said.

"Oh, boy!" Alvin shouted, and he jumped up and down so wildly he knocked a pitcherful of lemonade all over his best jeans.

That night, everybody went to the ball game. Willie Flashner hit a single, a double, and a home run to make up for his error in the first inning, and the Phillies beat the Mets, ten to three. Everyone stuffed himself at the game, so even Marty had a good time. And Alvin got not one but three special Phillies bats. He swapped three hot dogs for Marty's. And he bought Annie's for twenty-six pennies.

The rest of the trip was fun, too. Marty wasn't nearly as obnoxious as he used to be, and he didn't cheat at Monopoly even once. The bottled fireflies died from the heat, but Alvin got to see all the sights he'd planned on and quite a few he hadn't, and he spent two dollars and fifty-six cents plus tax on a replica of the Liberty Bell that turned out to have been made in Hong Kong.

Annie often got tired and cranky from all the walking they did, but she always cheered up when she got to play with Lambie the Second at the end of the day. And she learned to count by ten by practicing on the bites Lambie's fleas gave her.

All in all, Alvin and Annie agreed it was the best vacation the family'd ever had. The only thing she ever complained about was the loss of Lambie Number One. And the only thing that disappointed Alvin was the fact that the Mint didn't give free samples after all.